THEIR GREATEST

Power Surge: The Billionaire Club 1

Dixie Lynn Dwyer

MENAGE EVERLASTING

Siren Publishing, Inc.
www.SirenPublishing.com

A SIREN PUBLISHING BOOK
IMPRINT: Ménage Everlasting

THEIR GREATEST TREASURE
Copyright © 2014 by Dixie Lynn Dwyer

ISBN: 978-1-62740-865-3

First Printing: March 2014

Cover design by Les Byerley
All art and logo copyright © 2014 by Siren Publishing, Inc.

Printed in the U.S.A.

PUBLISHER
Siren Publishing, Inc.
www.SirenPublishing.com

DEDICATION

Dear readers,

Thank you for your continued support. I hope that you enjoy this new mini series about the true meaning of love. Each story penetrates the minds, the beliefs, struggles and presumptions of ten very wealthy, powerful men. They all realize that money can't buy you everything, and especially not the love of the perfect woman.

To fall into lust, unemotional love affairs, and maintain power and control of one's soul and assets is one thing. But, when faced with the deep and pure emotions of the heart, that power, that money means nothing.

True love is the greatest treasure of all.

Happy reading!

Hugs.

~Dixie~

THEIR GREATEST TREASURE

Power Surge: The Billionaire Club 1

DIXIE LYNN DWYER
Copyright © 2014

Prologue

Nash Riley walked into the club. He was trying to be discreet, but that wasn't going as planned. A glance to his right, and he saw an underage girl. She had a martini in one hand and was using the other hand to manipulate the bouncer, Frank, who should have been watching the bar area.

In annoyance he glanced to the left, and there was a small argument beginning between two patrons trying to get closer to the stage and the sexy little dancer doing her short act.

"Mr Riley? How are you, sir? I didn't know that you would be here tonight? Is everything okay?" Lou asked.

Nash bit the inside of his cheek. "Where the fuck is Riker?" he managed to squeeze out through clenched teeth.

Lou's eyes widened, and he knew the shit was about to hit the fan. Their employees were fully aware that Nash expected discipline and perfection. Riker, on the other hand, left in charge for the last two weeks, had let the ball fall. Riker was obviously too busy drinking and partying to get his act together, and now it could cost them big-time. He shouldn't have left. Nash shouldn't have gone out to upstate

New York to help their friend Peter. But Peter was good people. He was honest and fair.

Nash was getting tired of his twin brother Riker's blasé attitude with their club, The Jewelry Box. Fucking Riker was always partying and getting down with the ladies. This was their club, their investment. In the last year, it had turned to shit. The clientele came here to find easy women, and easy women came here to land some deep-pocket men.

Nash heard the explosion of voices. Women screamed, and as he turned, he caught one guy by the shoulders as the other man decked him. Nash ducked and bobbed, using his boxing abilities to evade getting hit. As a survival fighter, he'd never lost his touch. Even though he felt old and exhausted, he wasn't even forty yet.

"Lou!" Nash yelled then shoved the man toward Lou, and now Frank appeared and grabbed the other guy.

As Nash turned, some wild woman with a nasty right hook struck him. He roared in annoyance, and before he could let his temper flare, another bouncer, Bret, grabbed the woman by the hair and restrained her.

"Get them out of here. Clear the whole fucking place!" he yelled and then walked toward the bar.

John, the bartender, a nice guy, handed Nash a towel with ice in it.

"Here you go, boss. That was a hell of a move you pulled. I thought you were a goner when that big guy swung at you."

Nash raised one eyebrow at John, as if his assessment of what could have happened was a joke.

"Yeah, right."

Nash looked around the small club. It was turning into a shit hole. He didn't like the people who frequented it. He didn't care for what the place was turning into. He was going to need some help. He should call his good friends Jett and Flynn. They owned The Phantom, a restaurant and club. They knew people who helped with things like this.

"Hey, brother, what's the long face for?" Riker asked as he stumbled into the bar area with a blonde on his arm and a redhead standing behind him with her arms wrapped around his midsection.

Nash gave him a dirty look. He knew that Riker drank too much. They had both gone through a tough time. The one woman they loved was dead. She was taken from them because of their pasts. Once secret operatives for the government, hired out on a job-to-job basis, they did things they would never even let cross their minds again, never mind tell another person. They lost her because of those missions. They lost everything.

"What's going on? Look at this fucking place. Will you look around and see the shit that's going on around here? I don't want this, Riker. This isn't what we agreed to. This is not the place we talked about having. I'm tired of the losers coming in here. We need a fucking change."

Nash stared at Riker and held the cloth, filled with ice, against his lower lip. Then he tossed it onto the bar.

He watched Riker peel the women off of him, tap their asses, and tell them to take off.

Nash looked at his twin. They were nearly identical, aside from Nash's small scar by his left ear. A battle wound from his past career.

Most people couldn't tell them apart if they were dressed the same. But they didn't dress alike. Nash was more conservative, and liked a nice designer dress shirt and dress pants. Riker preferred designer jeans and tight T-shirts that showed off their similar athletic builds. Riker also had a more approachable expression. Nash didn't appear approachable, ever. He was hard, angry, and kept his contact with people limited. He preferred it that way.

"Did something go wrong at Peter's?" Riker asked, taking a seat next to Nash at the bar.

"No. I wasn't expecting to come back to some joint amidst low-class bars. I thought we discussed cleaning house before I left."

"I tried, Nash. Really. But, The Jewelry Box just isn't so attractive anymore."

Nash stared at Riker. He looked like shit.

"When was the last time you slept?" Nash asked him. Which was kind of hypocritical considering that Nash hardly ever slept.

"I got enough sleep. Don't you worry," Riker snapped at him.

Nash just raised one eyebrow at his twin.

"We need to do something or we might as well sell," Nash stated firmly. He looked around at the few stragglers that Frank and some other staff were escorting out. It was eleven o'clock on a Friday night. This sucked for business.

"Can we talk about it tomorrow? I've got plans," Riker said.

Nash stood up. He gave his brother a poke in the chest. "You need to straighten your ass out. You need to quit boozing it up and sleeping around."

Striker gave Nash a shove back. It turned into a match, back and forth, until finally they started laughing.

"You're an asshole," Nash stated.

"You're a bigger asshole who needs to get laid," Riker replied then plopped down onto the barstool. Nash glared at him and shook his head.

He didn't do casual sex. He tried it once months ago, after the two-year anniversary of Maggie's death. It didn't go well. Every night, and even during the day sometimes, he thought of them. The faceless men who identified Nash and Riker as secret agents and then went after Maggie. Nash and his brother should have died on that boat that night. They never found the men responsible, and never figured out for certain who they were. Riker had his suspicions, but even his suspicions were like phantoms in the night. They couldn't prove anything, and they couldn't bring them to justice as planned.

"When was the last time? And your hand doesn't count," Riker continued to tease. Nash stared into his eyes. The exact same dark blue color, and Nash could see the sadness amidst the words coming from Riker's mouth.

"I'm a little more discreet and particular than you, Riker. It has to mean something."

Riker lowered his head then ran a hand over the small dusting of whiskers covering his face. "When it's meaningless, it's easier to not feel and still get off. I'm going to head upstairs."

"I'll take care of everything here. Tomorrow, I'm calling Jett and Flynn. We need some help."

"Whatever."

Nash watched his brother leave. Nash felt just like Riker did. Except Nash wouldn't have sex just to do it. He missed Maggie. He missed her scent, her laugh, and her innocence. They were the reason why she died. They killed her, and he and Riker would have to live with that fact, forever.

Chapter 1

Chastity Malone stood in front of her boss, Colt Morgan, as they waited to see an acquaintance of Jett and Flynn Greyson's, who owned The Phantom, nightclub and restaurant. Now that place was phenomenal. She stood in front of Colt, discussing the reason for the meeting and the fact that two bachelors, Nash and Riker Riley, were looking to redo their night club, The Jewelry Box. She would never even think of stepping into such a club on her own personal time. It was a haven for perverted men looking to get lucky and women who drooled and opened wide for men with deep pockets. And boy, did the Greysons have deep pockets. They were wealthy, and so were their close friends. That was a group of individuals she would never fit in with.

Chastity led a boring, conservative lifestyle. She made sixty thousand dollars a year working with Colt Morgan, and that was just fine with her. She didn't date. She didn't trust men, and surely, she didn't have the ability or the flow of money to invest in things like owning a nightclub or seducing a billionaire.

She respected those who worked hard for their money, just like she did.

She had heard a lot about Nash and Riker. Colt warned her that they were difficult to deal with and that Riker had a bit of a drinking problem.

The door shoved open with a roar of laughter, as two gorgeous, sexy men entered. Following them were two other incredibly good-looking men, Jett and Flynn Greyson. She had helped them improve the restaurant part of their club, The Phantom.

"Hey, what's going on?" Colt asked as each of the men shook his hand.

Chastity tried to calm her breathing. The amount of testosterone in the room, along with the muscles and good looks, was nearly overwhelming. Sexy designer-shirt-covered perfection stood around her. Suddenly she felt insecure and obsolete. These were four billionaires. All in one room, and all around her, smiling.

Yikes. Down girl. You can handle this.

"Who is this?" one man asked as he looked her over. She immediately saw that look in his eyes. She'd seen it before. She thought she was unaffected by such looks, but not from him. The man gave her goose bumps everywhere. This one had to be Riker. Colt warned her that he was a complete flirt.

"Riker, meet Chastity Malone," Jett Greyson said then winked.

The others chuckled.

"Chastity, huh?" he asked then smiled. He reached for her hand, and when their fingers touched, he appeared affected. She felt that zing of attraction, and if she could, she would have given herself a swift kick in the behind.

"Hello, Chastity, I'm Nash Riley. It's nice to meet you," Nash said.

Riker immediately released her hand, but the reprieve was short lived as Nash took her hand next. Their eyes locked, and once again she felt a zing of attraction.

Not good. These men have reputations. They like to share women for crying out loud. Stay clear. Stay focused. Do your job.

"Nice to meet you both." She pulled her hand from Nash and his odd, surprised expression. Suddenly, he looked pissed off.

"So, Chastity and I would like to know what exactly you two have in mind for The Jewelry Box?" Colt asked.

"Well, we need changes to be made. We're not happy with the clientele or the staff."

Chastity took out her leather binder and notebook and took notes. She crossed her legs, pushed her long, blonde hair over one shoulder, and then fixed her skirt. She realized that the room went silent, and when she looked up, all four men were watching her, and Colt cleared his throat.

"The first thing we need to do is visit the club. We'd like to see it during the day, and then at night. We'll need access to your staff, the security you have, and the kitchen," Colt stated.

Chastity swallowed hard. Riker was in a dead stare at her.

She felt self-conscious now. *Is this what these men do? Do they stare at a woman like barbarians, and then decide if they want to make a move? Perhaps they shop for women like they shop for expensive cars and yachts and shit like that. Oh God, why am I shaking? Why is my pussy clenching? Well, you know why. They're beautiful.*

Riker and Nash were nearly identical, but as she watched them explain their likes and dislikes about their club, she saw some major differences in them. Riker was fast. Like a Bugatti Veyron, Riker was very fast. He liked instant, and no connections. He seemed ready to move on to the next thing as he added his comments then looked at his watch repeatedly as if he were impatient to move on to the next place. His eyes were a beautiful bold blue color. They stood out on his handsome face, as much as his very firm lips. He seemed arrogant, yet had already made several jokes that got them all to laugh.

Nash, on the other hand, was like a Ferrari, or perhaps even a Jaguar. He seemed discreet, conservative, yet debonair in his designer blue dress shirt and designer dress pants. His shoes were Fendi or some kind of high-end designer shoes. He had a small scar by his left ear. He looked right at her, and his dark blue eyes bored into her, making her turn away. But even as she scribbled some notes on the paper, she could see his face, and had already memorized his features. These twins could give any sane woman palpitations. She glanced at them again and found herself undressing them with her eyes. Boxers of briefs? Or perhaps, nothing at all.

Hell, what am I thinking? These men are all billionaires. They can have any woman they want. That fact alone is disgusting. Men like this are pigs. I don't need that type of aggravation. Look what happened between Desi and I. The man can't take no for an answer and is still hounding me to get back together. Like that would happen. I don't even know him anymore. Hell, I never really knew Desi, and as he showered me with meals at fancy restaurants and beautiful things, I never dug deeper, or asked questions about his success. He simply told me he was born into money. God, I was so stupid.

"I have to admit, I haven't been to your place," Colt stated.

"How about you, Chastity? You're in your twenties. I'm sure you and your friends have gone to The Jewelry Box," Jett said. She jerked her head up, surprised and caught off guard at them including her in this part of the conversation. They had just been discussing the entertainment and how their ideas about solo performances started turning into near strip teases.

She looked up at him and then heard Riker.

"No way she's ever been there. I would have remembered her." He leaned back in his chair and looked her over like she was a piece of meat.

She figured now would be the best time to let him—*them*—know where she stood. She leaned forward. "I never went there. I wouldn't even think about going there."

"Why is that?" Riker asked.

"Honestly?" she replied, holding his gaze.

He looked at the others then back at her. "Yeah."

"It's a place for men looking for easy women, and easy women looking to land a man with deep pockets. You're on display like a side of beef at the local steak house, and the food, I hear, is terrible."

"What? Is she for real? Are you kidding me?" Riker asked, raising his voice. Nash pulled his arm back and stared at her, too.

"No, Riker. We asked for honesty, and we're looking to change the entire atmosphere there. Go on, Chastity, explain what else you believe to be wrong with the place."

She swallowed hard. Although Nash's words were coming out calm and monotone, he appeared really angry. The lines by his eyes stood out more as he held her gaze and looked her over. Those damn goose bumps moved along her thighs, and as she adjusted her sitting position, the hem of her skirt bunched up slightly, revealing more thigh than she would have liked. Casually, she pushed the material down as she responded to Nash.

"It's not so terrible," she began to say.

"See. She's doesn't even know the place well."

"Oh, I know the place. I know to stay clear of it. You want to know what else? There are holes in the ladies' room walls that connect to the fifth stall in the men's bathroom. Anyone can go in there to see."

"What?" Nash stated as he stood up.

"I'm just telling you what I heard."

Jett and Flynn Greyson started laughing.

"You're in bigger trouble than you two think. Thank goodness Chastity and Colt are amazing. Look what they did for The Phantom when we lost our lead chef," Jett said.

She nodded her head. "That was tough."

"Sure was, beautiful, but you pulled it off," Jett replied then winked at her.

She felt her cheeks warm. Jett was a wild man, who hit on her a few times, but more so because that's what he did with every single woman he met. His brother was just as wild and often had women flaunting themselves at him. It was a bit too much.

"What are you doing tonight?" Riker asked her. Her heart immediately raced. She looked at Colt who seemed just as caught off guard. Nash stared right at her.

"Why?"

"Write down your address. I'll have our driver pick you up about seven. He'll bring you to the club. Then tomorrow morning we'll get together to go over your findings," Riker stated.

"I'll get there at eight. No need for your driver to pick me up," she said with an attitude. Now Riker and his rich-boy mentality were getting on her nerves. Did he expect her to swoon over him?

"Okay. I'll have to meet you there a little later, Chastity. I have that thing to handle for you," Colt stated. She widened her eyes. With these men surrounding her, she clearly forgot about Desi's cousin needing some insight at his bar across town. He had called her, but she thought it was a scam to get her to talk with Desi. She wasn't biting. However, it seemed he truly wanted Colt and her to look at his place and make suggestions, so Colt would go. She would work on things from the office.

"Sure thing. Thanks."

"Well, gentlemen. I guess we'll see you tonight," Colt said then rose from the seat. Chastity began to fold her notebook up, and as she stood, she dropped her pen. Jett and Flynn were walking Colt out.

"You really think that our place attracts those types of people?" Nash asked.

She looked up, surprised that he was so close to her.

He seemed insulted, and that wasn't her intention. Riker just rubbed her the wrong way.

"I didn't mean to insult you."

He raised his hand up for her to go no further. "I can handle the truth. Just be honest and assist us."

"I will, Mr. Riley." She began to step away.

She felt a hand on her arm and paused. Her entire body went into protective mode.

Riker stared at where his hand was, then released her.

"You don't have the job yet. This is a test. We don't throw around our money from our deep pockets."

She realized that even Riker had taken her comments to heart.

"That's okay, Mr. Riley. I haven't said that I accept the job if it's ours yet, either." She walked away and heard the low whistle behind her. They obviously weren't used to working with professional women who succeeded in business by working hard and not spreading their thighs.

* * * *

"Wow. That is one hell of a woman," Riker stated as Jett and Flynn closed the office door.

"You two had her attention. But be warned, she is definitely not easy," Jett stated.

"You tapped that?" Riker asked, and Nash gave him a dirty look.

"No. She's not that type of woman. She's classy, sophisticated, and conservative," Jett explained.

"Really? I think uptight and in need of some action."

"Cool it, Riker," Nash said.

"Hey, this is between the four of us right now. I know the others are a bit concerned, too. What's up with the heavy drinking lately and banging all the women? You have a death wish or something?" Flynn asked Riker.

"He'll get it under control," Nash replied then gave Riker a dirty look. Nash could tell that Riker was shocked. But he also smelled like alcohol and it was late morning.

"I'm good. We'll change the club and I'll change my bad habits. Now, you're sure you two didn't take Miss Virginity to bed?"

"She's too good for that," Jett replied.

"She works really hard, Riker. She had a bad relationship. The guy was an asshole. Colt had to step in to help her since she doesn't have any family around. So be nice," Flynn stated.

Nash wondered what happened. Instantly the thought that someone could hurt such a beautiful young woman bothered him.

Then came that wall of ice. Why should he care? He just met the woman.

But as they guys started talking about their weekly poker night in the back room at The Phantom, he could still smell her perfume lingering in the air.

Her long, golden-blonde hair was gorgeous. She had stunning blue eyes, the color of the ocean, and a smile that she didn't give too often but was worth the wait.

Instantly thoughts of Maggie entered his mind. He couldn't see her face. For a moment, he couldn't remember what she looked like. Then he saw Chastity.

He was aroused. Not just a mere attraction to a gorgeous woman, but an intense reaction from his body. He felt it in the seam of his pants between his legs. That surely never happened before. His belly felt tight with anticipation of seeing her again. *What the hell is wrong with me?*

Chapter 2

"I have nothing to say to you, Desi. It's been over between us for months. What is it that you don't understand?" Chastity asked over the cell phone as she stepped into her high heels. She wore a very simple black dress. It was elegant and sexy in a very classy style. She couldn't go to the club dressed like an office manager. She would stand out like a sore thumb.

"You know that we were good together."

"Oh really? That's why I found you in bed with that woman Celta whatever."

"Celetia. She's from Brazil."

"I don't give a shit. You made your choice when you had sex with her. Live with it. Good-bye."

She disconnected the call. She felt the frustration along with that bit of hurt ease its way into her heart. Desi had hurt her so badly. It had taken until just recently to start exploring the possibility of dating again.

What hurt the most about breaking up with Desi, besides finding him in bed with Celetia, was that she allowed him access to her desires. She trusted him. He'd betrayed her trust and now ruined her ability to give another man a chance. It didn't help that Desi had her followed either.

That night after work with Colt they'd grabbed a nice dinner and discussed their new clients. They were bouncing ideas around, and then Desi showed up and made a scene. She shook her head. The embarrassment she felt knowing that her boss, her good friend Colt, knew she had an ex-boyfriend who stalked her was horrible. But then

Colt stepped in. He protected her and got Desi to leave her alone and to give her space. Colt was so pissed off at her for not telling him how bad things had gotten.

But now Desi was starting to bother her again. She didn't want to tell Colt. He would totally freak out. Desi had been away for a while on some business trip. Involved with a business she knew nothing about, because the man evaded her questions. He wanted to know everything about her, yet Desi wasn't willing to share anything about himself. He had a cold, heartless look about him sometimes. It was like he would get lost in thought, or in another place, and then suddenly snap out of it.

His behavior had worsened, months after their casual dating. He became possessive, and she had that uneasy feeling in her gut each time he exerted a show of possession and ownership. She didn't like it. For weeks, for months, she contemplated breaking things off with him, and then she didn't have to. The son of a bitch cheated on her with that Brazilian goddess. The woman's boobs were so fake and so big they looked distorted. Chastity's were real. They were large, but not too large for her small frame.

Her phone rang again, and as she looked at the caller ID, she saw that it was Desi again.

She grabbed the phone and her purse, along with her clipboard, and headed out. Perhaps a night out in a club would be enlightening. Staying home, keeping the doors and windows locked, and listening for every strange noise, was getting old. If Desi kept this up, she would have to tell Colt, and maybe contact the police, for that order of protection.

* * * *

The Jewelry Box was crowded tonight. But now both Nash and Riker were seeing it through different eyes.

"She said meat market. Does it really look like a fucking meat market in here? Does she have any idea how much money we spent on those booths with the privacy curtains?" Riker asked.

"I think that was her point. Those curtained booths turned into private sex booths, and we both know it."

"Shit, Nash, I fucking know that. Damn, I've used those booths. Not for sex of course. Just to fool around a little. Loosen up the ladies."

"You're an ass."

Riker laughed. He reached for a shot that the bartender placed on the bar. Riker swallowed it quickly, and then placed the empty glass back down.

They both turned toward the doorway. Nash's chest tightened.

The woman in question entered the room. Chastity was wearing a sophisticated-looking dress that showed off her every curve, yet enticed the eyes with just a smidgen of cleavage from what appeared to be one hell of a rack. Nash immediately noticed the men checking her out, and damn did he just feel a burst of protectiveness and possessiveness come over him.

"She stands out like I don't know what," Riker whispered.

"Like a woman with class?" Nash replied.

"Not a side a beef?" Riker asked sarcastically.

Just as she spotted them, she placed her hand over her heart as if surprised to see them standing there, watching her. But before she could make her way toward them, one of the many men moving in for a closer look took her hand and spun her gently toward him.

They couldn't hear what the guy said, and that didn't matter, because Riker and Nash were in front of the guy in a flash.

"Take a hike. She's with us," Riker stated, and the small crowd dispersed.

"You okay, Chastity?" Nash asked her.

"Yes," she stated then turned away from him. "So, is this the typical crowd for a Friday night?"

"Pretty much," Nash replied.

"Well, I'll assume that you've told your staff about Colt and I coming here tonight. Do we have their full cooperation?"

"Yes," Riker stated this time.

Nash stepped a little closer to her as he led her toward the bar area. He inhaled her perfume. Once again, taken by the soft, light scent. It was very appealing. Her blonde hair was pulled back into a half-up, half-down style that accentuated her features. She had a lovely jaw that led to plump, sexy lips. When she poked out her tongue to lick the lower one, he imagined tasting her and drawing in that tongue to his own mouth. Shocked at what was an instant desire for the woman, Nash cleared his throat then ran a hand through his hair. He turned to look around the room. He needed to stay clear of her, and of these sudden emotions. No woman drew him away from his thoughts of Maggie or how he failed her. He couldn't get involved with another woman, even if he wanted to. He couldn't offer her protection. He had failed as a man, a lover, and a federal agent.

"What are those?" she asked with a clipboard in hand and a pen in the other. Her expression was more serious now. Her nose was scrunched up and she looked cute. That was so crazy. He never liked cute before. Maggie wasn't cute. Maggie had been a seductress.

Just then, as Nash looked toward the direction she was pointing, he spotted the booths. The curtain opened, and a woman was re-buttoning her blouse, her lipstick smeared on her face, and her skirt pushed up to her waist still.

"Those are something I came up with. You know, for privacy?" Riker stated very seriously as he stared at Chastity.

"Nice. So I guess allowing a prostitution ring to be run in your club is acceptable? Do you charge extra for use of the booths?" she snapped at Riker as she scribbled on her paper and then looked up, glaring at Nash's brother. Riker stepped toward her, whispering, "What the hell are you talking about? There's no prostitution ring here."

"If you charge for use of the booth, and you are aware of what's taking place behind them, then you're liable. Pretending ignorance to it won't work. Tell that to the judge and see if you get out of it. The booths and curtains go." She wrote a note on the paper on the clipboard she held.

Nash touched her arm as he stared down at her. He was a tall man. Over six feet two with wide shoulders, so he was definitely intimidating.

"Are you sure that's necessary? Perhaps a decision shouldn't be made now while you're feeling insulted."

"Insulted?" she asked.

"Well that's not what we're about. Those things happen in every club, and in some places, certain things are condoned."

"Let's move on. We'll come back to the booths later," she said, appearing flustered at Nash's touch. Was she attracted to him, too?

As she turned, Riker whispered next to her ear. "Later, with you in the booth, sounds promising."

Nash gave Riker a look.

* * * *

Initially, Riker was trying to frazzle Chastity. She was tearing apart their club, and most of all, she wasn't even responding to his pickup lines. He was annoyed now. An hour into the evaluation, and he stood by the doorway in the kitchen, leaning against the frame. She bent slightly to look under the stove grills then to check out some of the appetizers that were going out to the bar area. The woman had an amazing body. Her ass was fucking perfect. The material of her dress clung to every curve. She was definitely what he would consider voluptuous.

Other women he had been with recently hardly pleased him. This woman would be the bomb. He just knew it. But as he thought about getting her into bed, Riker felt a rush of guilt. She wasn't like that.

Not by a long shot. Suddenly, he felt a bit unsatisfactory and that shocked him.

He stared at the definition in her neck, then the dip of her shoulders, and her soft skin and breasts. He imagined touching her there, and stroking her skin. Then he saw her look at her cell phone and ignore the call again. Someone was trying to call her, and she obviously didn't want to speak to them. Maybe it was a boyfriend. He felt his disappointment. Maybe an ex-boyfriend?

"Stop staring at her as if she's a piece of ass on the menu," Nash whispered, giving Riker a nudge.

Riker leaned into his brother. "Like you're not interested in tapping that." He nodded his head toward Chastity, just as she bent over to pick up her pen.

A glance around them, and they weren't the only men checking Chastity's assets out. Riker cleared his throat and chuckled. Nash gave the evil eye.

It was interesting that his brother seemed attracted to Chastity, too. He hadn't looked at any woman since Maggie. Unlike Riker, who knew he was on a path of self-destruction.

"Riker, did you hear Chastity?" Nash asked, and Riker nodded his head, although not a word had been heard. He was too busy adjusting his stance. His cock felt so hard from staring at her. She wasn't even naked, and his body wanted in.

They all heard her phone vibrating as they stood in the hallway outside of the kitchen.

"Aren't you going to answer that?" Nash asked, giving his expression of disapproval.

"I'm working," she replied.

"It seems important," Riker added.

"It's not," she retorted, and then Colt's phone rang.

"Excuse me a moment." He took the call, but not before giving Chastity a look. Her expression changed to one of concern and anger. She watched Colt walk a few feet away.

Riker's gut instincts kicked in. Something was up.

"So, depending on your budget and the allotted time you will allow for renovations, how does three weeks sound to you?" she asked as Colt returned.

Riker saw him place his hand on her shoulder and squeeze it. Chastity and Colt locked gazes, a silent, nonverbal understanding took place. Then she lowered her eyes and he released his touch.

Were Colt and Chastity an item? No, they couldn't be. Sure, Colt was a big guy, and sort of good looking, Riker supposed. But were they lovers? That didn't sit well with Riker at all.

"So, give us a time frame that you can close down," Colt stated.

"You mean close the entire business down? For how long?" Nash asked. "Chastity just mentioned something about three weeks."

"Well, we could probably get a larger crew in here faster and get it all done. But it will cost you," Colt stated.

"How much are we talking?" Riker asked, but kept his eyes on Chastity. Her phone began to vibrate again. Colt looked at her.

"I'll take care of this and set it all up if you need to take that call."

"I don't want to. I don't need to."

So she didn't want to talk to whoever was calling her. Interesting. Colt seemed to be aware of the situation, and he looked concerned.

As they went over pricing and some ideas of a time frame, Chastity's phone was vibrating. She must have thought that turning it to vibrate wouldn't bother anyone.

"Maybe you should just answer that so we can focus on this?" Nash suggested with attitude. Riker chuckled. It was bothering Nash, too.

"Excuse me a moment." She pulled the phone off the clipboard and walked a few feet down the hall. There wasn't much room, and they could hear what she was saying. Riker and his brothers had always had superb hearing. It helped in their line of work as agents. So they listened to her call as they listened to Colt's ideas.

"You're drunk and I don't want to talk to you. No. I'm not at my apartment, and I don't want to see you. No, don't drive in your condition. That doesn't mean that I care. I'm working. Well, I know it's late, but some of us have to work for a living. We weren't born with silver spoons in our mouths. I'm hanging up now and turning off my phone."

Riker could hear the frustration in her voice. He got the gist of it. She didn't like drunks or men with a lot of money. So, he probably shouldn't have been downing the shots in front of her, and hell, he was filthy rich, but it was earned not inherited.

He stared at her back, and could see her taking a few breaths before she turned around and walked back toward them.

"Everything okay?" Nash asked. She nodded her head, straightened out her shoulders, and began to ask some questions as she submerged herself into her notes on the clipboard.

They worked out a schedule for renovations. They would all meet in two days to go over some ideas for a new place, a rebirth, as Chastity called it. It seemed that she would be heading the project, which meant more time getting to know who she was, and ultimately, getting her into Riker's bed.

He smiled. This was the first woman to ever ignore his advances and he looked at her as a challenge.

This is going to be fun.

Chapter 3

"You need to cut this shit out. If you don't let go of this woman, you could blow everything," Luke stated as he paced Desi's penthouse apartment.

"I can't. I can't get her out of my head. She's so beautiful and sweet."

"You fucked her, you had months with her. If she was so incredible, then why did you cheat on her?" Luke retorted.

Desi ran his hands through his hair. "I fucking lost it. I was drunk out of my mind. You know what the past two years have been like for me. I'm the reason why she's dead."

"Fuck that shit! Maggie knew what she was in for. She fell for those two assholes. She was supposed to con some money out of them and move on, disappear. She shouldn't have been there when the bomb went off. I'm telling you. She was trying to warn those two fuck heads," Luke stated.

Desi slammed his fist down on the table. "She didn't love them. She was using them. She needed the information to take down Reynolds. That agent and his team have been trying to catch Ferguson for three years. Working for the government as an agent, he was getting too close to screwing the operation, and that means we would all lose everything. Ferguson is our boss. He's the one who makes the decisions. Maggie knew she was supposed to manipulate the Riley agents. She did her job. It's part of the hazards of work like what we do. Plus, she was Ferguson's cousin. She wasn't our family, our blood, and seeking revenge is Ferguson's job."

"I don't see it that way. Those two assholes live, they nearly destroy the operation, and I lose Maggie. Then in the process, I meet a fucking angel, and I screw that up. I'll get my chance at revenge, for myself, for Maggie, and for Ferguson. I know they live here in New York. I've been at bars and clubs they've been at. They're going to die eventually." Desi downed another shot then coughed as it burned his throat.

"Alcohol will destroy even the greatest of men, Desi. But take it for what it is. You're a crook, a thief, and a gambler. You were running a farce with Chastity. You were pretending to be a different person than who you really are. Focus on the goals here. Another six months, and we can retire and live in a mansion on the beach in some other country. Chastity wouldn't fit in with that. That's the difference. She would have left you the moment you told her the truth."

"The truth?" Desi whispered.

"Yeah, that you kill government agents who interfere with drug smuggling operations for our mob boss, Jose Ferguson. You infiltrate high security areas, investigate individuals to find their weaknesses, and then move in for the kill. It's our lives. So forget about that fairy-tale ending with Chastity. The moment the woman finds out about who you really are, that you kill people for a living, she'll hate you, and then you'll have to kill her." Luke popped a piece of gum into his mouth as he leaned against the couch.

Desi stared at him in anger and disbelief. Desi wanted Chastity in his bed. He wanted her beside him as he took her to the finest restaurants and catered to her every whim. He'd fucked up, and his splitting headache was a reminder about drinking too much and about losing everyone and everything that meant something to him.

I'm not giving up. I want you in my bed, Chastity. You belong with me. Nothing else matters.

* * * *

Nash and Riker entered the back room at The Phantom nightclub. It was owned and operated by two of their buddies, Jett and Flynn Greyson. They shook hands with their other friends.

"Heard you guys are finally cleaning up house," Emerson Pierce stated as he shook Riker's hand.

"Yeah, I guess you could say that." Riker took a seat at the poker table.

"I heard that Colt Morgan and his staff were doing the job," Emerson's best friend Stone Ryder said.

"Sure did. They're the best around and came highly recommended," Nash replied then gave a smile to Flynn.

"How's it working out with Chastity?" Jett asked, just as Riker tossed a jalapeno popper into his mouth.

"Damn, these are good." Riker took a sip from the beer he brought in with him.

"Chastity came up with those. A personal recipe. You know, a sweet, crispy coating on the outside, and a warm, spicy center on the inside. Sound familiar?" Flynn asked then winked.

"Who's this Chastity?" Zane Heston asked.

"Yeah, sounds intriguing, Riker," Cash Corbin added then dealt out the cards as they all gathered around the table.

"She's assisting with the rebirth of The Jewelry Box," Nash stated then leaned back in his chair.

"Oh, a rebirth, huh?" Emerson teased.

Riker shook his head, and Nash smirked.

It never got old, messing around with these guys. They were their best friends, all knowing one another since grade school, or in the field as agents.

Cash and Zane owned and operated numerous security firms and also bought out companies and rebuilt them from the inside out. Like the rest of them at the table, Cash and Zane were billionaires.

Hudson and Jagger were like Nash and Riker. They were twins and worth billions. They lived on the wild side and never took anything seriously, except when their friends were in trouble or in need. They were family. They were also two of the biggest men Nash knew. They were about the same height as Nash, but built like football players. They were quite intimidating.

"So, are you both sleeping with her yet?" Stone asked as he placed the first bet down on the table.

Stone and Emerson were best friends and complete opposites. Stone lived on the wild side and didn't care about anyone's opinion or point of view. His best friend, Emerson, was more discreet. He was usually there to pick Stone up after one of his crazy stunts that, more often than not, got Stone in a heap of trouble.

"No. She's very nice and very professional," Nash replied.

"What does she look like?" Stone asked.

Jett pulled out his cell phone. He scrolled the screen then handed his phone over to Stone.

"Holy fuck. Listen, guys, I'll be more than happy to stop by this week and perhaps see how the renovations are coming along," Stone said as he stared at the screen and licked his lips.

"She is one fine-looking woman. You say the name is 'Chastity,' huh?" he teased. Then Zane pulled the phone from him.

Nash listened to their comments, their whistles, and their compliments on how sexy and beautiful the woman was.

"She's a perfectionist, Stone, so you wouldn't get along with her," Riker added.

"She's uptight, huh? There's ways to deal with that. You know, loosen her up," Jagger added, and they laughed.

"She's not like that. Let's just hope this process goes smoothly, and we have a better place to show for it when all is done," Nash added.

"And perhaps a woman in your bed to share," Zane replied.

They were all silent. He looked up and stared at them.

"Come on now, you know it's what each of us want but haven't found. Perhaps, it will work out correctly this time," he added.

Nash threw down his cards.

"What's that supposed to mean, Zane?"

Zane never really cared for Maggie, nor did the other guys, but they were supportive.

"Nothing, Nash. Forget it. Let's play. This is poker night, and women talk is off limits until we hit the club outside those doors," Zane said, but Nash felt angry. Riker and Nash cared for Maggie. Her death had killed them inside, and he couldn't understand why their best friends never really trusted her.

Chapter 4

Chastity didn't dare step up to the highest rung on the ladder to see if this colored bulb made the custom light fixtures stand out more. She stood on tiptoes as she twisted the bulb into the fixture. The other workers were in the adjacent room, and she couldn't bother them just to insert these bulbs. Right now she was over the table of the booth she'd redesigned, minus the curtains. If she lost her balance and fell, at least she would hit the table and booth seats, instead of the stone tile flooring.

"Oh shit," she said as she began to lose her balance while trying to hold the fixture and insert the bulb. It seemed that someone hadn't screwed in the fixture base completely, and now, it was moving. The hand-blown stained glass fixtures were shaking as she held on to one of the three thin poles they descended from as well as the bulb.

Instantly she felt the large hands on her waist.

"Don't move. I got you."

She nearly jumped out of her skin from the feel of Nash's hands on her waist.

She glanced down at him and took a deep breath as she absorbed his casual attire. Dark blue T-shirt, designer, she was sure, and blue jeans. Her belly did a series of flip-flops and then came the embarrassment of being caught like this. Add in the fact that her low-rising jeans needed to be pulled up, her belly was exposed, and that she was probably flashing her thong right now, and yeah, humiliation was hard to swallow.

"Can you let go of the bulb and fixture?" he asked, holding her by her hips.

"Not exactly. It seems that one of the workers was a bit rushed and didn't screw in the base tight enough. If I release this now, we're going to have a mess on our hands. These fixtures are expensive."

"Your safety is more important, Chastity."

"Just go grab one of the guys and he can get a screw driver and fix this while I hold it in place."

"I'm not releasing you. You'll loose your balance and crack your head open."

"What's going on in here? Did she finally say yes to trying out the booths?" Riker asked as he entered the room.

"Riker, really?" she reprimanded, then nearly lost her footing. He really got her temper flaring. "Hold still, Chastity." Nash raised his voice, and his grip was strong on her waist. She felt his warm fingers against her very sensitive skin. Her nipples hardened and her breasts tingled. God, she was so sexually attracted to these men. But why? They were totally not even her type at all.

"What do you need?" Riker asked, and Nash told him to grab a screwdriver from one of the guys.

"Just send one of the workers in here. Ask Bobby to come in."

"He'll get it," Nash stated, and she felt his hands move ever so slightly on her waist. She swayed slightly, and he gripped her snugly. "Don't move around so much."

Riker returned with a screwdriver in hand.

Chastity removed the lightbulb with one hand then handed it to Riker. She then took the screwdriver, reached up higher, and screwed the screws in tighter.

All the while, she felt her entire body shaking with these two men watching her and staring at her backside.

"Is that a tattoo?" Riker asked as she finished tightening up the base of the lighting fixture and could finally lower her arms. She felt his fingers against her skin, and she jumped, turning toward him.

Luckily Nash was holding on to her still.

"Whoa!" Nash stated, and she climbed down the ladder, pushing his hands from her waist the lower she got.

She stepped aside immediately and stretched out her arms, bending them then flexing them. They were stiff.

"Sorry about that. So what do you think?" she asked, trying to change the subject.

"I like it," Riker said but didn't take his eyes off of her.

"Good. I know they're a bit pricey, but I think they add a classier ambiance to the booths. I have a surprise for you guys. I hope you like the idea. It won't take a lot to maintain, but it's definitely unique." She ran her hands across the smooth granite of the table.

"Okay. What is it?" Nash asked, crossing his arms in front of his chest.

"Do you see these lines?" she asked, and both men leaned forward to look at the square cut out they hadn't noticed before.

"Press that button on the side of the booth wall."

Nash pressed the button, and slowly the center square in the table opened. It revealed a small grill, on coals.

"What is this?"

"Kind of like a hibachi grill, right in the table. It is run by propane and the control panel is right here. The heat is low, and doesn't cook the food, but rather, warms it up and keeps it hot. The kitchen servers would special deliver a platter of prepared items. Grilled shrimp, chicken, and beef on the skewers, and a few other specialty items. It will be ordered by the platter, and it's part of sitting in these specialty booths."

"Holy shit, Chastity, I'm impressed," Riker stated, and she smiled, feeling relieved that they liked it.

"Good. The plan tomorrow is to actually have you both experience what it will be like in your new place, Hidden Treasures."

"Hidden Treasures?" they both responded at the same time.

"Yes. Colt and I feel like the name of the club should change with the rebirth of the place. You need something unique and classy. This is the new place, the new clientele, and the new staff, for the most part."

"Hidden Treasures, huh?" Riker asked.

"No," Nash responded.

Chastity was surprised at Nash's tone. "Why?" she asked.

"No. The Jewelry Box has meaning."

"Nash, she's gone, and really, we never liked that name. It wasn't how we envisioned our place," Riker replied.

Chastity wondered what they meant by "she's gone."

"Why don't you two discuss it? I think you'll find that the name is just as important as the changes and what is now being offered here. Throughout the restaurant and club there are hidden treasures. Just like this table with the hidden grill, there are other secret compartments around. Some offer tokens for free drinks or discounted meals, and others offer gorgeous pictures or illusions to be admired. You'll see tomorrow, as you both get to experience some of the things we're working on. I'll leave you two alone, and I'll be in the kitchen going over the recipes for the new menu."

* * * *

Nash ran his fingers through his hair.

"What the hell is wrong with you? I kind of like the name," Riker stated.

Nash turned to stare at his brother as if shocked by his statement. Riker was checking out the grill.

"That name was Maggie's idea."

Riker looked up from the grill. "No it wasn't. She wasn't even into picking out a name. She threw that one out there and you grabbed onto it."

"It's all we have left of her."

"It's time to move on, Nash. It wasn't like we were married to her."

"You never could admit that you loved her. You always held back."

"Fuck, Nash, I'm not having this argument out with you here in the middle of the fucking club. You want to get it all out? Then fine, let's go upstairs and talk about it. She controlled you. She wanted to have sex with both of us, and it was good. Did I love her? I don't know. When she died, because of that fucking case and no-name, no-face drug operation, was I pissed off? Hell yeah. She was beautiful, and we shared a lot of time together, but she's dead. Two fucking years, Nash. I think it's more than time to move on."

Riker walked away and Nash stood there filled with annoyance.

He stomped toward the kitchen, but as he entered, there was Chastity with the new kitchen staff mixed with a few of the old ones, and she had their full attention. He heard the excitement in her voice and saw their enthusiasm toward her ideas. She was a gorgeous woman. There was no denying the attraction, and holding her on the ladder was torture. The scent of her perfume and his dick shoved hard against his zipper demanding release was crazy.

Perhaps if he were finally able to let go for a bit, he could see himself letting go with Chastity.

Chapter 5

Chastity was sitting at the bar with Adelina. She was the club manager for The Phantom, and they had become friends while Chastity redid the menu.

"So, tell me the truth, how difficult is it to work for Nash and Riker?" Adelina asked.

Chastity took a sip from her martini. "They're fine."

"Honey, they are more than fine. Those two hot men are sought after by so many women. Riker is such a ladies' man, and his twin, Nash, a total silent, brooding type. The ladies go crazy for them when they come around on Wednesday nights."

"They come here on Wednesday nights?" Chastity asked, realizing that was what tonight was. Her expression must have revealed her interest and concern as Adelina laughed.

"You like them, huh?"

"No. Absolutely not. Been there, done that. Men with money, good looks, and women practically throwing themselves at them is not my type at all."

"It was your thing months ago. Desi is an attractive man."

"Don't bring that asshole up. He has been hounding me to get back together."

Adelina took on a serious expression. "Is he stalking you? I mean harassing you? Because I know people."

Chastity smiled. "I can handle it. I just don't know why he keeps coming around. He cheated on me. I would never take him back. Besides, his friend Luke creeps me out. I swear I think Luke is into something dangerous and illegal."

"That wouldn't surprise me at all. So how is the remodeling going over there? What's the new place going to look like?" Adelina asked, just as Jett came up behind her.

"Hey, Adelina, we're going to be in the back for a bit, could you let me know when Natalie gets here? I'm going to need to cancel our date tonight."

"Sure thing boss," Adelina stated as Jett let his hand caress along her waist. He winked then walked away.

Adelina remained staring at him.

"When are you going to make a move?" Chastity asked.

"What?" Adelina looked back at her pretending as if she didn't know what Chastity was talking about.

"You like him."

"I like Flynn, too. That's the problem. They both aren't attracted to me."

"Why not take a chance?"

"And risk getting fired? I don't think so. Those two pay good money."

"I bet you're wrong. Maybe just getting some alone time with them would help."

"I've been alone with them, Chastity."

"Helping them into their beds upstairs after they've drunk too much is not alone time. Or helping them to dodge their lovers either."

"I don't help them dodge their lovers."

"Oh, really? What are you going to tell Natalie when she shows up?"

Adelina shrugged her shoulders. "Nothing. I'm not making a move. I'm not assertive like that."

Chastity completely understood her friend's fear. She lived with that every day.

Adelina reached to her waist and turned toward the bar as she began to speak with one of the employees a moment. Her cell phone was somehow connected to every employee in the place as well as to

Flynn and Jett. It was awesome technology, created and installed by Jett and Flynn's friends, Cash Corbin and Zane Heston.

"Chastity?" She heard the voice and her entire body immediately went into protective mode. The nauseous, tight feeling in her belly and the fear gripped her insides.

Turning slowly, she locked gazes with Desi.

"I thought that was you. How are you, baby?" he asked then went to bend down to kiss her cheek. She moved to the side, causing him to stop, mid motion.

"What are you doing here?" she asked.

She looked at him. Bloodshot eyes, six feet tall, wide shoulders and deep brown eyes. His chiseled face gave an appearance of maturity and intensity. She wondered why she had fallen for his charms. He was a good-looking man, but he was a liar and a cheater. She needed to remember that.

"The question is, what are you doing here? This isn't exactly a great place for someone like you." He reached up to touch a strand of her hair. She pushed his hand away.

"Please leave, Desi. I don't want to cause a scene." She started to turn in her seat when he leaned over her back, placing his arms on either side of the bar, around her. She was closed in. His scent and his dominance were intimidating and scary. She feared this man. She got that instant creepy feeling whenever he was this close to her.

"Then don't cause one. Come with me. We'll go somewhere where we can talk."

"No."

"Chastity, is everything okay?" Adelina asked, holding her fingers to the earpiece. Chastity knew she was talking with security or someone who could intervene.

"Yes. Desi was just leaving."

Desi stared at Adelina. "Give us a minute, doll. Chastity and I have something to discuss."

He leaned forward and sniffed her hair, giving her the chills. When he gripped her shoulder hard, she tensed up and gasped. The warm breath against her ear sent shivers over her body.

"This isn't over. You can do this the hard way, but I guarantee, it won't be pretty, Chastity. Be smart. Come back to me and we'll work it out. Come on now. Let's go."

"No." His threats and his tone brought tears to her eyes.

"Is there a problem here?"

She turned to see Jett and Flynn Greyson, along with two bouncers.

Adelina crossed her arms in front of her chest. "I do believe that this gentleman was just leaving. Alone," she added with attitude.

"Sir, if you'll please exit along with these gentlemen, it would be appreciated," Flynn stated firmly.

Desi caressed Chastity's hair and whispered into her ear, "I'll be in touch."

He stepped back and gave Flynn and Jett the once-over.

"I was just leaving, and it has nothing to do with you," he said then smirked at Jett and Flynn as if they were diddly-squat.

Chastity watched Desi walk out with the two big bouncers following him. Adelina grabbed her hand and touched her shoulder.

"Are you okay? Did he hurt you when he grabbed your shoulder?"

"He touched her?"

They both turned to look at Nash and Riker. Riker looked pissed off.

"Oh God, how embarrassing." Chastity turned away.

"It's fine. Don't be embarrassed," Adelina stated.

"I think I should go now," Chastity whispered.

"No. Not yet. He could be waiting by your car for you. Who is this guy, Chastity?" Flynn asked. But when she looked up, Riker and Nash were moving closer and now stood directly in front of her. They stared down into her eyes, towering over her even though she was sitting on the high barstool.

"Who is he?" Riker asked.

"Riker, give her some space. We can have her escorted home in a little while. Let's be sure to give the guy time to get the hell out of the area," Flynn said.

"We'll take her home," Nash stated.

"I'll drive her car, and Nash will follow," Riker said.

"No. Absolutely not. Flynn, call Colt. Tell him that I need him."

"Colt? You're seeing him?" Riker asked, sounding annoyed.

"Listen, this is embarrassing enough. Please don't ask me questions. You're clients. It stops there." She slid down off of the barstool. She fixed her skirt, and then she saw him reach for her chin and slowly looked up, locking gazes with Riker. Did she want him to touch her? He was just being concerned. She must have looked fearful, because he pulled back.

"Did he touch you?"

This was so not appropriate. *God, I'm making a mess of things.*

She took a deep breath and turned her face slowly away from him. But he stepped closer and placed his hand on her hip as he leaned his mouth toward her ear.

"You're shaking, and I know he scared you. You can trust us."

She felt Riker's fingers stroke her hipbone and then he released her, and then stepped back. He must have sensed her uneasiness after Desi's harassment.

Now Nash was standing beside her looking her over.

The sexual tension between the three of them was phenomenal. Two of the sexiest, best-looking twins she'd ever laid eyes on were staring at her with concern and desire. She knew that look, and it shocked her that it was double and that she was aroused by the possibilities.

"Hey, Colt is clear across town. It will take him over an hour to get here. Can you stay put? Or do you want to go to his place? He said that you know the code to get in," Flynn stated.

Both Riker and Nash looked upset, but they stepped away from her.

She took the reprieve even though Flynn's statement made it sound like she did have a thing going on with Colt. That was the bit of space she needed.

"Let him know that I'll be at his place. Waiting for him." Flynn widened his eyes and stepped away as Nash and Riker just stared at her.

* * * *

Nash didn't know why he was so aggravated and disappointed that Colt and Chastity were an item. He hadn't dated in years, and hadn't slept with a woman in just as long. So why was he gripping the steering wheel so tight as he drove Chastity to Colt's penthouse? He wished he knew what Riker was thinking. But he couldn't ask him. Instead he stole a peek to the passenger side of the Range Rover and saw Riker staring straight ahead.

When they arrived at the building, the doorman knew Chastity, and she knew all the codes to get into the place. She was quite familiar with the elevator code for the penthouse suite, and then the code to get inside.

She walked through the main living room area and clapped her hands to illuminate the room.

Turning around to face them, she had a look of pure fear.

"Well, thank you for driving me and for following me up here. I'm good now. I'll just wait for Colt to get here." She took a step toward them.

Nash still couldn't believe that she was with Colt. Colt seemed so not her type, and also not very macho. Maybe it was just jealousy.

"Maybe we should wait until he gets here," Nash said then walked deeper into the room.

"No. You should go. I'll be fine," she said, turning toward Nash as he passed her and headed to sit down.

"Who was that guy at the bar? Ex-boyfriend?" Riker asked her then took her hand and moved closer to her.

Nash watched, wondering if his brother was actually going to make a move. They knew Colt. He was a friend of Flynn and Jett. That was also besides the fact that they stood in her boyfriend's penthouse and waited for his arrival.

"I told you not to worry. It's none of your business, Riker."

Riker reached up and touched her cheek. She stepped back and lowered her eyes. Riker placed his hands on his waist.

"I'm worried, Chastity. He was a big man and he hurt you."

She shook her head.

"He did hurt you. Jett and Flynn brought you up on camera in the back room where we were."

"We saw him grab your shoulder." Nash moved in behind her. He slowly reached down and touched her shoulder from behind her.

Chastity flinched.

Riker widened his eyes in anger.

"The fucker did hurt you."

"Please, Riker. This isn't right. I'm embarrassed enough as is. This isn't any of your concern."

Riker placed his finger over her lips.

"The moment I saw his hands on you, the second I witnessed him hurt you, and saw the fear on your face, it became my business."

Nash stepped closer to her back. He pressed his body snuggly against hers.

"And mine, too."

She shook her head as if trying to deny the attraction they were feeling.

Could she not feel the chemistry between the three of them? This is what he and Riker had wanted to have with the perfect woman. He had thought that Maggie was the one, but after Riker's admission days ago, Nash realized that Riker didn't feel the same way.

"Please. I don't want to cause any trouble. I'm working for the both of you."

"Don't you feel the attraction between us?" Riker asked.

She took a deep breath and then released it.

"Yes, of course I do. But Mr. Riley, it wouldn't be—"

Riker cupped her cheeks between his hands and stared down into her face. "I think it's time you start calling me Riker."

"Oh God. This isn't a good idea. Colt will be here any minute."

"It should take him at least another fifteen minutes or so to get here," Riker said.

"Are you seeing him?" Nash found himself asking. He was shocked at how pissed-off he got, just thinking that she was with Colt.

"It's really none of your business."

"We're making it our business," Riker added.

"Is this what you two do? You push your way into a woman's business and try to seduce her to do what you want? I'm not falling for your flirtatious ways, Riker. I saw the club and the booths. You said they were your idea. Maybe that's the type of women you're used to. I'm not like that."

"Chastity, you have no idea who we are or what we're made of. Does our experience intimidate you?" Riker asked as he stroked her one cheek with his finger. He trailed it down her lips, then to her throat.

"Riker?"

"Can I kiss you, Chastity?"

"Riker." she whispered and he leaned down, and as his lips came closer, she closed her eyes. She wanted to feel his lips on her. She wanted to see if this attraction to him and his brother went deeper, just like Riker hoped it did. She allowed it, and he made his move, giving her the time she needed to turn away or turn him down.

Nash watched as Riker leaned down and began kissing Chastity.

* * * *

Riker didn't know what came over him. Her perfume, her sexy dress, her classy body, or perhaps the fact that some shithead tried to hurt her? He wasn't sure, but he knew he had the urge to protect her and to get to know her in every way. He wanted her under him, naked and in his bed. He wanted to run his fingers through her golden locks and get lost in her blue eyes. He wasn't even drunk. Except, maybe drunk on his attraction to Chastity.

He delved his tongue deeper and felt her hands against his chest as he explored her mouth. He kept a hand against her lower back and used his other hand to cup the back of her head.

He wanted to imprint his kiss in her mind and to her soul.

She moaned softly, and it was music to his ears. Then he felt her pulling back, and he knew she needed to slow things down. As they parted lips, he locked gazes with her and the soft, swollen lips he'd devoured moments ago.

"Damn, woman, you sure are tasty."

She shyly looked down and kept her hands against his chest.

Then Nash used the back of his hand and knuckles to caress her cheek. She turned toward him, and Riker could feel her shaking.

"I haven't kissed a woman in a long time, Chastity. It's been forever," he admitted, and Riker's chest tightened. His brother had suffered terribly when Maggie had died. It took months to get him to join civilization again. He truly felt at fault.

"I've never been kissed like Riker just kissed me. Two men have never kissed me consecutively. It's unnerving."

Nash brushed his fingers across her lips then cupped her face between his hands. Riker watched as they locked gazes, and Chastity didn't pull away.

Nash slowly leaned toward her then covered her lips with his. He pulled her from Riker's arms, and Riker released her with a smile.

* * * *

Nash wanted all of her. He wanted to get lost in her kiss, in touching and exploring her body. It all came to him at once, like some secret assault, catching him off guard.

He delved his tongue deeper, felt her moan into his mouth, then pulled her curvy body against his own.

He cupped her ass with his hands and squeezed her to him. But then the sound of the elevator leading to the penthouse ruined the moment.

Chastity pulled from his embrace and panted for breath. She covered her mouth with her hand and shook her head slowly side to side.

Nash felt just as affected and overwhelmed. "Chastity?"

"Please. That can't happen again. I can't allow this."

The doors to the elevator opened, and there came Colt, and he looked angry.

"What happened? Did he hurt you?" he asked, approaching Chastity quickly. She ran to him, meeting him halfway, and Colt hugged her.

Nash felt his insides twist into a knot. What had they done? What the hell just happened?

"It's okay, baby. He can't hurt you. I'll protect you," Colt stated then locked gazes with Nash and Riker. "Thanks for taking care of her."

"No problem. We'll see you tomorrow at the club," Riker said with an attitude.

As Riker passed Chastity, she turned to look at him and her expression was blank.

"See you tomorrow, Chastity," Riker said.

"Yes. We'll see you tomorrow," Nash added then they entered the elevator.

Nash noticed that Colt looked at Chastity, then he looked at them, and the man was shooting daggers at them. The doors closed.

"Fuck!" Riker stated then banged his hand against the elevator wall.

Nash remained quiet. He had enough to deal with, with his own reaction here. That kiss, those lips. "That definitely can't happen again."

Riker just stared at him with anger in his eyes.

* * * *

"Okay, so what happened after Desi was escorted out of the club? What happened between you, Riker, and Nash Riley?" Colton asked.

Chastity stared at him a moment. Colt was her best friend and one of her only friends aside from Adelina, who she'd only met months ago.

She covered her face with her hands.

"They kissed me."

"Wow! You go, mamma. Not one, but two dangerous, intimidating, and sexy men. I could have told you that they were interested since meeting them at Flynn and Jett's office."

"Cut it out, Colt Morgan, or I swear, I'll tell Carlisle that you have a thing for him."

Colt raised one eyebrow in the most adorable way then gave her that look of his. "No one has figured out that I'm gay but you. Carlisle is not for me anyway. He's too gay."

Chastity laughed out loud. "This coming from a man who has more high heels than any other woman I know."

"Oh…please. I hardly ever dress in drag. It wouldn't go over well with the majority of my clients if they knew the truth."

"That's because the majority of your clients have been macho, heterosexual males. Why put yourself through such torture?"

He shook his head. He looked so serious suddenly, and she didn't mean to upset him.

Colt was strong and had great masculine qualities, but he just preferred men over women.

"I'm sorry," she said then cuddled up next to him on the couch.

He pulled her legs onto his lap then pulled off her heels. "So, are you staying for a while again?"

She took a deep breath then sighed. "I don't want to impose."

"No. You stay. Desi is getting worse. His actions are definitely psycho level. Let me call in a favor to some friends."

She started to decline the offer, but he began tickling her toes and then her calves. "Agree!" he demanded, and in between his tickling tactics, she agreed.

"Fine. Fine, do it. I just don't want another scene like tonight to happen in front of the Rileys. They're our clients, and it was so unprofessional tonight. I was completely embarrassed."

She leaned back and crossed her arms in front of her chest.

Colt leaned back, too. "Honestly, Chastity, I've known you for three years now. Don't lie to me, and don't lie to yourself. You like the both of them."

She stared into his big brown eyes, and knew that she could trust him. He was her best friend.

"The attraction is there, but two men at once?"

He fanned himself then chuckled.

She laughed, too, and gave him a playful punch in the arm.

"It's very common. It's not like they do it all the time. I know these things. I've got connections."

"I'm sure you do, but I don't do these things. Desi was my first real boyfriend. My first lover."

"But, he didn't make you orgasm, remember?" Colt teased then wiggled his eyebrows.

"Thanks for reminding me. I didn't even know what that was. I mean I totally thought it was pretty good."

"Yeah, but what about with Riker and Nash. They are carrying some big guns, and if I can be so bold to say, they are smoking hot."

"I could come from their kisses alone," she whispered, leaning back and closing her eyes.

"Is that what I walked in on? Hmm. So what's the game plan for their club tomorrow? We have a lot to go over with them."

"I'm not sure that I'll be there. Perhaps remaining in the background, doing the ordering, and helping to pick out the paint and décor would be better?"

"You can hide from the truth for only so long. Maybe they're trustworthy, too?"

"I can't think about getting involved with another man, or two, even if I wanted to. I don't know what Desi is capable of."

Colt pulled her against his side and held her in his big strong arms.

"That's what I'm afraid of. Let me talk to my friends and see if we can keep you safe until we can get Desi off your back."

"I really don't want anyone to get hurt."

"Don't worry. These friends of mine are very resourceful."

Chapter 6

Cash Corbin ended the call and looked at Zane Heston.

"I can't believe it. Colt really thinks that this Desi guy could hurt Chastity," Zane said.

"I get the feeling that Nash and Riker are interested in her. The way they reacted last night at the club was a definite indication," Cash stated.

"I know. I was kind of happy for them. Nash took Maggie's death hard. It was a crazy night, and he blames himself for her death."

"I know. But the truth of the matter is that she's gone, and he needs to move on."

"Riker moved on pretty quickly," Zane said then laughed.

"That crazy son of a bitch."

"He's not going to be too happy when he finds out that Chastity hasn't gone to the police."

"Colt said something happened back at home, in Charlotte, where she's from. It probably has something to do with that."

"New York is a definite change from the Carolinas. But she fits in just fine. She's a very attractive young woman."

"She sure is. So, let's help keep her safe. I think we should handle this one personally," Cash stated.

"Sounds good to me. I'll see what I can find out about this asshole Desi. You start with the surveillance on Chastity. Colt said she lives in a crappy apartment building. We're going to want to get better security for her there. Chastity is not going to make this easy on us. Colt already warned me."

Zane nodded his head and smiled.

"That's why you're so good with the ladies, Cash. You'll get her to cooperate."

"Hmmm. I don't know. Maybe we should just let Riker and Nash assist."

"Retired federal agents? They could do more damage than good."

"They could make Desi disappear, and we wouldn't have to do all this leg work."

Cash laughed. "You're spoiled, Zane. Get to work. My father wants to meet for dinner tonight."

"Oh no. Who does he want you to help now?"

"Not just me, but us. We're a team, remember?"

"How can I forget, when you remind me all the time?"

Cash laughed. "Well, I think this situation might pull at your 'wannabe commando' strings."

Zane turned to look at Cash. His expression immediately interested.

"Dangerous?"

"I sure as shit hope not. But, you know I like that, too. We'll know more after we meet Mr. Costiano."

"Mr. Costiano? As in owner and operator of one of the largest seafood distributors in the Northeast?"

"You got it."

"Interesting."

Cash winked, but the truth of the matter was he was concerned. His father, Bradford, believed that Mr. Costiano was in danger, and so was his family.

* * * *

Chastity had to go back to her apartment. She took a shower at Colt's and now needed to change for work. He of course headed to Riker and Nash's club to prepare for tonight. She was accompanied by Zane and Cash, two friends of Colt's as well as Flynn's and Jett's.

She was a bit embarrassed to show two billionaires where she lived, but as they drove toward the apartment, never asking her directions or for an address, she realized that they already knew. She clasped her hands on her lap and couldn't help but worry about a thousand things. Who were these two men? What were they capable of? How did they know Colt? What if Desi were there at her apartment, waiting for her? Should she really get an order of protection? Wouldn't that irritate Desi?

As the SUV stopped in front of the complex, she noticed the unmarked police car as well as two other men dressed casually but wearing dark glasses. They pointed toward the SUV and nodded, as if giving an okay.

Cash, with the brown eyes and sexy personality, turned to talk to her.

"Okay, honey. It's all clear to go up to the apartment. Zane and I are going to escort you. After you get dressed and ready for work, Zane will drive you to the club."

"Oh, I'm not going there. I was going to run some errands with one of the assistants."

Cash squinted his eyes at her.

"Listen, plans have changed. You'll be safest at the club with Colt, Nash, and Riker watching you."

Even the sound of their names aroused her and made her feel nervous. She couldn't see them. Not after last night. Not after their kisses.

"Chastity, whatever is going on between you, Riker, and Nash—"

"Nothing! Nothing is going on. What do you mean? Why would you think that?" she asked, clutching her bag on her lap.

Cash looked at Zane and Zane shrugged his shoulders.

"Okay then. Nothing is going on between you, Riker, and Nash. I got that. But your safety is most important here. You're going to the club. Colt can assign some people to do that other stuff. Now let's get out and head upstairs. The door was locked and we didn't want to force our way in. I'll stick around with the others, and secure your apartment better. Okay?"

She nodded in agreement, and instantly felt sick. Who the hell were these guys? Why were they taking an ex-boyfriend's threats so seriously?

She got out of the SUV and was escorted by Cash and three other men.

The moment she unlocked the door and entered the apartment, she knew that Desi had been there. She covered her mouth, and felt the tears reach her eyes. Then she felt Cash's arm around her waist.

"What is it?"

"He was here."

"What? The door was locked. There was no sign of him outside," one of the other men stated.

"How do you know?"

"I can smell his cologne. Can't you smell that musky, expensive perfume scent?" she asked.

The men inhaled.

"Yes. I can smell it. That's not the normal smell in your apartment?" Cash asked as the others moved through the small apartment and then went to the bedroom.

"Cash. We got something in here," one of the men said.

She started to walk that way when Cash stopped her. "Wait here."

She was going to refuse, but the truth was, she was scared. Maybe she didn't know Desi at all.

A few seconds later, the two men walked out of the room with no identifiable facial expressions whatsoever. She swallowed hard as they exited the apartment.

Cash walked out, too. He had a hand on his hip and a serious expression on his face.

"Honey, he was here. He was definitely in your bedroom."

She swallowed hard.

"What did he do? What did he leave?"

"Come here. But don't enter the room. I've got the guys bringing up a detective friend of mine from downstairs."

"Why?" She peeked into her bedroom, next to Cash, by the doorway.

The first thing she noticed was the new sexy lingerie in red lying on the bed. There were thigh-high stockings and red stiletto heels with rhinestones on them to match. The top had holes where breasts would go, and the thongs were missing one important frontal piece. She had never seen it before. But then she noticed the two large vases of red roses and that one side of the bed had been slept in or perhaps just laid on.

"That's not mine. He was here waiting for me. He got that for me to wear," she whispered, her voice cracking, and then tears rolled down her cheeks. She didn't understand why this upset her like this. Why did it creep her out so much? Why was she denying that there was a serious problem here?

Cash wrapped his arm around her waist and pulled her from the room as the apartment door opened and two detectives entered.

"Back there. Maybe you can get some prints," Cash told them.

"We'll have to ask the woman some questions," the other one stated.

"After. Just give her a few minutes."

The detective nodded his head and walked into her bedroom.

She felt so invaded and dirty. Why?

"Hey. Hey, look at me," Cash said then placed his fingers under her chin for her to look up into his eyes.

"It's okay. You were smart to stay with Colt last night. We're going to stop this guy from bothering you."

She couldn't even speak. It was like this wasn't really happening. She felt numb, and then Cash hugged her.

She didn't even know the man, but she held on to him as she closed her eyes and prayed that she wouldn't become a victim of domestic violence, like her mother had been.

Chapter 7

"What? Bring her to the club. Have her pack some things, Cash. She's staying at my place," Colt stated into the cell phone.

Riker listened as he stood by the bar. He and Colt were going over the bar menu and the new drink ideas that Chastity had. She was supposed to be here an hour ago.

Riker looked around for Nash but didn't see him. He wondered what the hell Colt was doing talking to Cash. What did he mean for her to pack clothes and that she was staying with Colt?

Riker got that instant feeling of jealousy, yet the woman wasn't even his or Nash's. Yet.

"I understand. Of course not. Who is the detective in charge? I want all the contact information. Yes, I'm taking this seriously. Okay, I'll wait here. Yes, Nash and Riker are around."

Riker waited for phone call to end. Colt looked legitimately upset, which hurt. This was crazy. Riker didn't even know the woman well. Hell, he lusted for her body, was enticed by her perfume and sexy good looks, but this was a bit much for him. What was with the instant possessive feelings?

"Is everything all right?" he asked Colt.

Colt rubbed his face then nodded his head. An instant lie.

"Lou, pour us two shots!" Riker yelled to the bartender.

The shots were poured and placed onto the bar.

Riker leaned against the bar and slid the full shot glass toward Colt.

"Have one. You look like you need it."

Colt looked up at Riker. He stared at him a moment and Riker could see such emotion. Colt really cared about Chastity. *I'm such a fucking dick. I want him to stay away from her. I want a shot at Chastity. I can't stop thinking about her lips, or the way she felt in my arms as I kissed her. Fuck.*

"You need to stop drinking," he told Riker then downed the shot and placed the empty little glass back down onto the bar.

Riker squinted his eyes at Colt as if there was more meaning to that statement.

"I like to drink. It calms me," Riker said and then downed his shot. He placed the glass onto the bar and held Colt's gaze.

"Some women don't like that. Some women fear a man's abilities, and control when he's had a few too many."

"I can handle my alcohol fine."

"You still have your connections with the government?"

Riker hadn't expected that question. He just stared at Colt. The man was spooked. He was angry and emotional about the call with Cash. Riker didn't like the feeling he had.

"Tell me what's going on, Colt. I can tell that you're upset."

Colt stared right back at Riker as Nash headed toward them.

"Forget it. Forget I even said that."

"Hey, what's going on? Are we trying these new drinks yet?" Nash asked as he joined them by the bar.

"I'd like to wait for Chastity. Can you guys give me a few minutes?"

Just then Chastity walked into the club with Cash by her side.

Riker took in the sight of her. Her toned legs accentuated by the black high heels and the long, sexy slit up the side of her little black cocktail dress. She wore a short champagne-colored shimmering shawl over her shoulders, which were bare from the strapless dress. It showed a slight bit more cleavage than usual but was still conservative. Then Riker locked gazes with her. Her eyes were glossy, the tip of her nose red, as if she had been crying, and then instantly his guard was up. But before he could react, Colt was rushing toward her and pulling her into his arms. Riker felt like someone had just punched him in the gut.

One look at Nash and he could tell that his brother was affected, too.

Cash walked over.

They each shook Cash's hand.

"How is it going? The place looks so different. It's really classy."

"Yeah, we're stepping it up," Nash replied.

"What's going on? How is she?" Riker asked.

Cash shook his head.

"This ex-boyfriend of hers is a serious problem," Cash said then turned toward Colt and Chastity. Chastity was walking toward them now and she didn't look happy.

"Sorry that I'm late. If you just give me a couple of minutes to check with the staff, then we can begin, before the crowd gets here," Chastity stated.

"What crowd? We're not opening," Nash replied.

She smiled. "Don't worry. Colt and I have about thirty people coming in to give their opinion on the new design of the place, the atmosphere, service, and food. It will give us some insight on whether we're headed in the right direction for your success." She smiled then excused herself.

"It's okay, Nash. Chastity knows what she is doing."

"Okay," Nash said then watched Chastity walk toward the bar. Riker noticed how Lou's eyes immediately lit up when he saw her. The other bartenders appeared happy to see her as well, and that just added to his misery.

"So, what's going on then? Are you going to let us in on the situation with Chastity last night?" Nash asked.

Riker waited to see how this would go over.

"Please respect Chastity's privacy. Myself, Cash, and the detectives will handle it. Excuse me." Colt headed toward the kitchen, where Chastity had just entered.

"Okay, what the fuck is going on?" Riker asked Cash.

"Why do you want to know?" Cash asked Riker then gave a smirk. *The fucker knows we're attracted to Chastity.*

Riker looked at Nash, who was pretending disinterest, but Riker knew better.

"She's a beautiful woman. She seemed very upset last night, and just now when she got here with you. If you're escorting her here, then something else went down," Riker stated.

"She stayed with Colt last night. She's staying with him tonight, too." Cash held Riker's gaze. Cash had such a dark way about him. His eyes were dark brown, his hair wavy, and he dressed like he was corporate but was capable of causing physical pain. Riker had known him for many years. He was a great friend and trustworthy.

"Nash and I care about Chastity," he slowly revealed to Cash. Cash, of course, couldn't accept just that as he raised one eyebrow at him.

"Is she in danger?" Nash asked very seriously. Even Riker looked at Nash, surprised by his particular question and the obvious concern. Was Nash thinking about Maggie again? When would he get over her and move on?

"I won't lie, but I must respect her wishes," Cash began to say.

Riker gave him a firm look. "We go way back. Our friendship, our connection is a hell of a lot stronger than your relationship with Colt and Chastity."

"Oh, pulling that shit on me, huh? You didn't let me finish, Riker. You're so fucking demanding."

"Like you didn't know that about him or me?" Nash added and held Cash's gaze.

Cash looked toward the kitchen and then around them.

"It's serious. She's in a bit of trouble with this ex of hers," he began.

Riker not only felt angry about the asshole bothering her and leaving the things he did at her place, but he also felt upset for Chastity. As Cash explained the situation, Riker knew that he wouldn't be able to stand back and let Colt take care of her. Colt didn't seem as if he had experience. Not like him and Nash did. But Chastity definitely trusted Colt. Would she learn to trust him and Nash, too? As he looked at Nash, he knew his brother was thinking exactly what he was, even though Nash was scared. He was scared of opening up his heart again, never mind touching another woman and sharing another woman. But the connection and attraction was there between them and Chastity. They needed to work out a plan. A way to get to know her better, and see where this relationship could go.

Just then Colt and Chastity walked out of the kitchen carrying the new bar menu and a tray of little appetizers.

Gaining Chastity's trust starts now.

* * * *

Chastity was trying her hardest to concentrate on explaining each drink as Lou made them. But it was difficult with Riker leaning over her shoulder, asking her questions about the menu and the descriptions.

The crazy thing was, she nearly completely forgot about Desi until her cell phone began to vibrate, indicating that a call was coming in.

Before she had a chance to look at it or move it off of the bar and clipboard, Colt grabbed it.

"Colt. What are you doing?" she asked as he answered the phone and walked away.

As if knowing exactly what was going on, Riker wrapped an arm around her waist from behind and held her in place.

His warm breath collided against her ear and neck, and instinctively she turned gently into his touch.

"Let your boyfriend handle it. This gives me the opportunity I've been waiting for."

What did he mean "boyfriend"? What opportunity? He thought that Colt was her boyfriend?

As she slightly turned her chin up toward him to ask him what he was talking about, Riker touched his lips to hers. He kissed her ever so softly, and it seemed to be a gentle peck, until he pressed his tongue between her lips and squeezed her body against his. She felt his erection against her spine. She tried to pull away, but her lips and her body had a different reaction. She reached up and cupped her hand against his cheek. She felt the masculine skin beneath her fingertips, as a rush of desire and sexual attraction pulled at her inner core.

She could hear Colt's voice rising. Something was wrong.

She pulled from Riker's lips. He released her instantly as Colt returned, and she wanted to tell him so badly to keep holding her. She was shocked at the instant need to be held by Riker.

Then she locked gazes with Colt. He was fuming.

"That motherfucker just threatened me."

"Colt, please. You shouldn't have taken the call." She reached for the phone, but Nash took her hand, turned her so that her back was against the bar, and caged her in. That delicious cologne of his filled her nostrils. The bulk of his manliness devoured her emotions, her rationale, as she stared up into his dark blue eyes.

"Tell us what's going on, and we'll help."

She shook her head then turned toward Colt.

Colt shook his head at her. "I'm sorry, Chastity, but I'm not going to lie. I'm worried about you. You're my best friend, and I love you, but this guy is crazy."

"Colt, please." She felt Nash's hand against her cheek, drawing her attention back to him. Now Riker stood beside her and placed a hand on her waist, too.

"You can trust us. Let us in on what's going on. Don't fight us."

She held her ground. She was determined to not be some damsel in distress, like her mother had been. Her mother ran away from one abusive relationship then back into another one that ultimately killed her. *Not me. I'm going to handle this alone.*

"You're clients. This is completely unprofessional. I don't need your help with this. It's none of your business." She could tell that Nash was clenching his jaw and biting the inside of his mouth. His anger, and the darkness of his eyes, made her gut clench with trepidation and sadness. She wasn't trying to insult him. She didn't even know these men well, yet she didn't want to insult them and push them away. Was she really attracted to them? Was she willing to take a chance at such a peculiar relationship? They were big, muscular men.

They have money, they have power, and God knows what else. What do I have but bad luck, five thousand dollars in my savings account, and one terrible past relationship that appears will haunt me for quite some time.

"Chastity, they can be trusted," Colt stated.

"Let me see my phone, Colt."

She felt Nash's hands move to her waist. He gave her hips a squeeze, indicating for her to focus on him.

She looked back up into his eyes. She felt his grip on her hip bones, and it made her feel feminine and aroused.

"Don't be scared. We're the good guys, and we want to help."

"Nash, please respect my wishes. Please stay out of this. I don't want or need your help in my personal life. Can we please just get back to the menu?"

He stared down into her eyes a moment, and something told her that this conversation with him wasn't over. But now that Lou interrupted, saying that the guests would be arriving in fifteen minutes and that they were behind schedule, Nash released her.

She immediately took her phone from Colt.

"We'll discuss this later," she told him then tossed the phone onto the bar where the clipboard sat, and she began asking Lou to start creating one of the drinks on the menu.

* * * *

An hour later, Nash stood next to Riker, watching Chastity interact with the guests. He had to admit that the woman had an innate ability to draw people in and get them to open up about the new club. The guests were scattered around different areas of Hidden Treasures and introduced to the new aspects of the restaurant and club. Overall, it was a hit. Each person rated the area they were in, the service being provided, and their overall feelings of the new name and the club itself. The papers were gathered and then surprisingly, Chastity revealed the ultimate surprise of the evening. There was a dance floor and new DJ area with a large aquarium as the back drop that added a final touch. Both Nash and Riker were shocked.

"Oh my God, is that a treasure chest?" someone asked as the guests explored the aquarium, and Chastity gave the signal for the music to start. Instantaneously, some of the crowd cheered and began dancing, getting the full effect of the atmosphere. While others walked over to their favorite spots, indicating to Nash and Riker that Chastity had been right about it all.

Riker moved in behind Chastity as she stood to the side and watched the guests. She had a smile on her face, and that in itself made Riker smile.

He gave her shoulder a little nudge with his arm as he stood next to her.

"A treasure chest with jewels coming out of it and a mermaid, too?" Nash took position on her other side.

"Well, I know how resistant you were to the name change. So I figured this was a compromise. If either of you don't like it, we could change it all. But that would mean the logo, with that sexy mermaid sitting seductively on top of the treasure chest, and the aquarium, the various shrimp, lobster, and crab meals on the menu, and the—"

Nash turned toward her and cupped her chin with his hand. She gasped. "You did amazing, Chastity. You're more than I imagined. The name, everything stays."

"So how about you, Chastity? Will you stay?" Riker asked. But before she could respond, Nash lowered his lips to hers and kissed her lightly. He whispered against her lips. "Friends first, Chastity. Thank you, for everything."

His heart was racing, but Nash was overwhelmed with attraction to Chastity. He thought about the bedroom upstairs, connected to their office, and about bringing her there. He could spread her out on the bed, and explore her body, with his hands and his lips. He never thought he could feel like this. But he knew she had fears. Hell, he had fears himself. Especially about the newest question that kept popping into his head.

Why did it never feel like this with Maggie? Did I imagine something more than was actually there?

* * * *

"I'm watching her right now."

"Who is she with, Karen?" Desi asked as he paced the hotel room. He had left this morning, early, for a business trip. He wouldn't be back until next week. He couldn't believe that Chastity was getting an order of protection against him. Like that would fucking keep him away.

"Well, there are two guys with her right now. Both big, both very attractive."

"Are they touching her?" he asked through clenched teeth.

"Well, they've been very attentive all night. But she seems resistant."

"How so?"

"Well, every time they whisper next to her ear or approach her, she tightens up. She looks tense."

"Who the fuck are they? I want you to find out who they are, Karen."

"That's easy, Desi. They own the place. They're twin brothers."

"A name?"

"Something Irish, I think."

"Find out, and let me know."

"Will I see you tonight, Desi?" she asked him, and his dick didn't even get hard at the prospect.

"No."

"I'll text you the name," Karen said, and then he heard the click as she disconnected the call.

Did she not get my intentions by leaving her the lingerie? I threatened that stinking, nosey boss of hers. I think Chastity needs a reminder about straying. She may need some time to think things through, but perhaps a little reminder that I'm in charge and she belongs to me will get her coming back sooner rather than later.

Chapter 8

"So what do you think?" Cash asked Zane as they stood in the room at The Phantom, waiting for the others to arrive. Zane was looking at his cell phone, rereading the text from the detectives.

"It seems like this guy doesn't do much of anything. He flew out to Miami. But nothing stands out. I don't know if I should have him followed there or what? It's like I have this feeling that there is more to this asshole than just him wanting Chastity back."

"I don't like it. We should pull in some favors, and get an ID on this dude's past. I'm worried for her," Cash said.

"Worried about who?" Jett asked as he and Flynn entered the room. They started to take their places around the large poker table.

"Chastity."

Jett and Flynn immediately looked up toward Cash and Zane.

"What's going on? What did you find out?" Flynn asked.

"Well, nothing, really. The detectives say the guy doesn't have a record. As a matter of fact, he's an upstanding citizen," Cash replied.

"Well, maybe he's obsessed with her, and it's sent him over the edge?" Jett suggested. Cash thought about that a moment as Nash and Riker entered the room. Everyone greeted them. Behind them, Hudson and Jagger entered.

"Where are Emerson and Stone?" Flynn asked.

"They got a little sidetracked by the bar. Two blondes, you know," Hudson said and they laughed.

"Who's obsessed and over the edge?" Riker asked.

* * * *

Riker heard Jett's statement, and something in his gut clenched. Then they got silent as Riker and Nash entered the room.

"Well? What's going on?" Nash asked.

"We were just talking about a case," Cash stated.

Riker looked at Nash as he took his seat and placed his glass of bourbon down on the green velvet.

"Are you talking about Chastity?" Nash asked.

Riker didn't like how Zane looked at Cash and then Cash took a deep breath and released it.

"She got the order of protection the other day, and that asshole was served the papers," Zane told them. Riker felt on edge.

"Who was with her?" he asked.

Emerson and Stone walked into the room, smiling and laughing.

"Getting lucky tonight?" Jagger asked them.

"Jealous?" Stone replied in his traditional wise-ass manner.

"Fuck you, Stone. I get plenty," Jagger stated.

"Not from what I heard."

They all laughed at the teasing banter except for Riker. He was worried about Chastity.

"So, Cash, what happens next? Any info on this guy harassing Chastity?" Riker asked.

"Chastity? Who the hell is that?" Emerson asked them.

"She's Colt Morgan's assistant. She's helping out Nash and Riker with their new place. What is it called now?" Flynn asked.

"Hidden Treasures. The opening is Friday night, so if you boneheads aren't busy, maybe you'd like to check it out," Nash said.

The others threw around some comments about seeing it. They made jokes about it being a dive, and about it failing, just to mess with Riker and Nash. Both of them smiled, and blew off their friends' wise-guy comments.

"So, this Chastity is hot. Is she going to be there?" Stone asked.

Riker gave Stone a very serious look and tried to not reveal how pissed off Stone's comment was making him.

"She'll be there, but she's not your type," Riker stated.

"Oh really? I like all types. Are you guys staking a claim?" Stone asked.

Riker looked at Nash and knew that Nash wouldn't say anything. Not yet. Not when he was still trying to get over Maggie.

"No, we're not. She's taken," Riker said.

"By whom?" Zane asked him.

"Colton," Nash stated, sounding annoyed.

Zane and Cash laughed.

"She is not dating Colton," Zane told them. The others just looked at Nash and Riker. Apparently their friends knew more than even they did.

"How do you know that?" Riker asked with an attitude.

"Because Colton is gay," Cash said. Nash nearly spilled his drink.

Riker looked at Nash, and although no words were exchanged, he knew his brother was thinking exactly what he was.

"So she's available? Good. I'll be there Friday night. Can't wait to meet her," Stone added.

"Just deal the cards," Nash told Stone as Stone smiled then began the game.

Riker was surprised that Stone would even want to bother with women for a while. Not after Olivia St. James tried to trick him into marrying her so she could take his money. That bitch had been suave and nearly got away with it. Luckily, Emerson saved his friend from the fatal mistake.

It seemed to Riker that Chastity wanted them to think that she was dating Colt, to stay clear of him and his brother Nash. They were going to have a talk with her as soon as she arrived Friday night.

* * * *

It was Thursday, and Chastity took the day off to visit the aquarium and clear her head. Desi left numerous messages, stating that he was away on business and that when he returned, they were going to have a serious talk. She was still angry at his tone and assumption that she would see him. Didn't the order of protection prove that she wasn't interested?

She pushed a strand of hair behind her ear and adjusted her sunglasses. That nagging sensation in the pit of her stomach kept reminding her about how familiar this all was. The never-ending phone calls, the threats, and demands were all indications of a stalker, a man who controls and batters women. But she didn't want to believe that this would happen to her. She didn't want to assume the worst about Desi since he never struck her or verbally abused her. It was like she had this label inside of her head about what a batterer really was. She took an uneasy breath and dismissed the nagging sensation once more. Today was a day of relaxation and peace.

It was a gorgeous, warm day, and the weather for Friday was going to be clear and mild. The perfect weather for an opening night for Riker and Nash's place.

The thought of them filled her with mixed emotions. She looked over the railing in the sea lion area, and watched the amazing animals swim beneath the water. There were a set of stairs leading underneath the tank where she could watch them swim below. She walked that way and entered as a couple exited.

She watched for a few minutes and enjoyed the underwater activity. Glancing at her watch, she knew that the underwater aquarium exhibit was just down the way, and she loved seeing all the sea creatures and assortment of fish. She headed that way.

Walking in the sun, she felt her cell phone vibrate and her chest tightened. This was the new reaction she had every time her phone rang or buzzed. She worried that it was Desi and that he would continue to make her life miserable. Sometimes she wondered if she should just meet with him one more time in a public place and make him understand that it was over between them.

She glanced at the message box. *Colton.*

Hey, are you still at the aquarium?

She texted back as she walked to the line for the underwater sea life exhibit.

Yes. What are you up to?

Just trying to get word out about the opening tomorrow night. Where are you exactly?

The aquarium underwater sea life exhibit. You know I love this place.

Great! Call me later and let me know how your responses are for tomorrow. We need a successful turnout.

No problem. Bye.

Chastity smiled to herself then walked along with the small crowd down to the underwater aquarium. It was huge and very beautiful. Most of the people walked through quickly, but not Chastity. Sure, there were other things to see at the exhibit, and even some new things, brought in each year, but the aquarium that remained all year round at the exhibit was her favorite. It was a thirty-five minute ride to get here, but well worth it. It made Chastity feel like she was getting away from it all. As she took a seat on one of the benches, hidden to the side of a little cove area, she imagined being in the tropics. Someplace warm and relaxing with white sandy beaches and not a care in the world. The reality of her life was that she could never afford such vacations. But here, even for just a little while, in her mind, she could pretend.

She watched the various tropical fish swimming through the water. There were so many different species. Maybe one day she could go snorkeling.

"Is this seat taken?"

She swung her head around the moment she heard Nash's voice. Surprised to see him here, she felt her jaw drop and then the second voice sounded on her other side.

"How about this one?" Riker asked, and she looked back and forth between them. They leaned forward and she leaned back so it would be easier to talk with them.

"What are you two doing here?"

"We came to see you," Riker said then smiled. She absorbed the sight of the tight dark blue shirt he wore and his designer jeans. A glance toward Nash, and she was surprised to see him wearing jeans and a nice navy-blue T-shirt. A Polo Ralph Lauren, by the label on the sleeve.

"What? Why? How did you—" She closed her eyes and gave a sigh of understanding. "Colt." She whispered.

Then she crossed her legs and leaned back against the bench.

What was that man thinking? She was trying to maintain some control and sanity here. Staying away from Nash and Riker was her plan. She just needed to get through opening night tomorrow. Then she wouldn't have to see them again.

"So, is this why you came up with the idea for our club? You like this stuff?" Nash asked.

She swallowed hard. She could do this. She could have a perfectly natural, platonic conversation and relationship with these two men. So what that her heart was causing her voice box to shut down? Maybe they didn't notice her nipples pressing hard against the white tank top she wore beneath the sheer white blouse.

"Chastity?" Nash whispered, and then Riker placed his hand over her knee but kept his eyes straight ahead as if he were transfixed on the sea life.

His warm, large hand felt so good against her skin. She felt instantly shielded from harm. Wasn't that a misconception?

She cleared her throat and tried to push Riker's hand off her knee, but he wouldn't budge. "Riker?"

"Tell me about how you came up with the aquarium idea?" Nash asked then faced her as he took her hand into his and held it on his leg. She looked down at it. She felt the excitement, the connection of having both men touch her at once. It was an amazing feeling. She had to look away from Nash. She couldn't look at either man's perfect face. It was too much. She felt too much.

She stared at the water in front of her.

"I didn't pick it because I like this stuff. I asked your staff what things interested you and Riker. After some deep research, and a bit of snooping around, I found out about your fishing magazines and snorkeling trips to Maui, New Zealand, and Costa Rica, Nash. I heard you enjoy going to the beach. And Riker, I found out about your love of collecting unique art, and a bit of a fantasy about mermaids." She smiled.

Riker squeezed her knee and Nash clasped her fingers between his fingers and gently squeezed.

"You are pretty resourceful," Nash said.

She looked at him. "I have to be. I have to gain an understanding of the client, so I can make their dreams and visions a reality," she replied.

Nash stared at her, and she looked up at him. She could get lost in the deep blue of his eyes.

"We didn't give you much to go on, yet you figured out what we like."

"Like I said, Nash, I asked your employees."

Riker moved his hand up her thigh to her waist, and turned toward her. He cupped her face with his hand and moved closer.

"Sounds to me like you interrogated them."

She was lost in his dark blue eyes, and how the color of his shirt brought out the blue. He leaned closer.

"It doesn't seem fair."

"What?" she somehow replied.

"That you know a bit about us, and we know hardly anything about you," Riker said.

She shyly attempted to look down but Riker wouldn't allow it. "Don't shut us out." He pressed his lips to hers. He kissed her softly as Nash squeezed her hand then moved his fingers and hers up under her skirt and against her skin.

Riker deepened the kiss, as Nash stroked his fingers and her own between her thighs. She kept her legs crossed and tightened up. Pulling from Riker's kiss, she panted.

"Oh God. What are you doing to me? We're in a public place," she stated.

"No one is coming over here," Riker told her very confidently.

"You don't know that. This is a public place. Anyone can come around the corner."

Nash stroked his finger back and forth against the *V* between her thighs and her panties.

"Honey, sometimes being naughty and fearing getting caught can be a total turn-on," Riker said.

Nash stroked her panties again. "It can be very stimulating." She was shocked. Nash was the conservative one. The un-wild twin, or so she thought.

"Oh God, this is crazy."

"It is, but trust us and we'll take care of you." Riker leaned closer and began to kiss her neck and then lick her skin. He cupped her breast and she gasped. Riker covered her mouth with his. He devoured her soft moans as Nash pressed his fingers firmly between her thighs. She was struck with a whirlwind of emotions. Desire, excitement, fear, lust, all consumed her. But she couldn't move. She could only react to the feel of their strong hands, the power of the kisses, and the safety of their arms.

She didn't want to resist. Her pussy felt so tight and needy. One touch. Just one stroke and she would shoot off this bench.

Nash leaned against her other side and whispered into her ear. "Open for me. Let me ease that ache, baby."

Oh my God, I want to. Oh, but I can't. Can I? Oh hell.

She slowly uncrossed her legs. The need to feel more of Nash's touch and to relieve the throbbing in her cunt was too much. Combined with the fear, the anticipation that someone may come into the little cove in the corner, aroused her. She wasn't an exhibitionist, but for crying out loud, she liked the feeling she had right now.

Her belly did a series of somersaults.

"That's it, Chastity. God, you feel so soft. These panties feel tiny. They barely cover you." Nash stroked along her slit. Back and forth, she felt her cream lubricate her cunt. Riker deepened the kiss, he stroked his tongue into her mouth, and then Nash pressed a digit up into her pussy.

She gripped onto his hand.

Nash kissed her ear then whispered next to it. "Release my wrist, baby. Let it go. Just feel. Damn, you're so wet. You got me so hard right now, Chastity. Fuck." Nash thrust a finger up into her.

Somehow he pulled one of her legs over his leg, instantly opening her up for his ministrations. Adding a second digit, he thrust his fingers into her very wet pussy.

She pulled her mouth from Riker's, and Riker continued to kiss along the seam of her lips, then the corners of her mouth, her cheeks, then back to her mouth again. It was like neither of them could get enough and neither could Nash.

His strokes deepened.

Riker smoothed a hand into her tank top and cupped her breast. She thrust her hips against Nash's fingers, and then Riker pinched her nipple. She moaned louder into his mouth. It was all too much for her. The fact that at any moment someone could catch them doing this excited her. Small spasms erupted from her pussy. Her own cum dripped down her ass. She felt her entire body tighten, and then Nash stroked another finger over her puckered hole and she lost it. Riker pressed harder against her as she nearly screamed from her orgasm. She felt herself lose her breath. Her vision clouded, her mind incapable of any rational thoughts. Nash slowly stroked her some more then eased his fingers from her pussy. He fixed her skirt and her thigh then kissed her cheek as Riker released her lips. They stared at her.

Riker pinched her nipple, making her gasp. "You are amazing." He kissed her cheek.

She felt her body heat up all over again. He removed his hand and fixed her top. She assisted him then leaned back and stared at the water display in front of her.

"So that's what an orgasm feels like?" she whispered.

Nash touched her cheek. He stared down into her eyes with a very serious facial expression. "You never had one before?" he asked. She was embarrassed once again in front of Nash and Riker. She swallowed her pride and figured that she already admitted it, so what did it matter now.

She shook her head. "Never."

Riker caressed his hand up her crossed thighs. "Oh, we're going to be giving you plenty of those." He winked then nipped her lower lip.

"Riker," she scolded then lowered her eyes. Both men grabbed a hand of hers and leaned back against the bench.

"So, how many little hidden nooks like this are at this exhibit?" Nash asked, and she shook her head, feeling her cheeks warm, as both men chuckled.

* * * *

Nash and his brother took every opportunity to touch Chastity or caress her skin as they toured the rest of the exhibit. When they came to a series of specialty designed paintings that were 3-D images or appeared to be moving images, he recognized the paintings.

So did Riker.

"Hey, this is the one of the moving mermaid in the ocean. It looks so real, and almost exactly like the one you had put in at Hidden Treasures," Riker said as he walked closer and started checking out all the different paintings from the local artist.

"I thought you would like that one. I had a hard time actually. Because there's this one, too." She pointed to a beautiful painting of a seascape and a mermaid sitting on a large boulder sunbathing as the waves crashed against the rocks. The wind was blowing her long blonde hair behind her, and she was smiling.

Nash stood behind her. He could see it clearly over Chastity's head.

"Hey, you look like her, Chastity," Nash said, and she shook her head in denial. Riker squinted his eyes and moved closer. "My God, Nash, you're right. It's beautiful," Riker said.

"Why didn't you choose this one?" Riker asked.

"I don't know. The other one fit better for the club. This one looks more like it should be in a study or a special place. It wouldn't be appreciated in the club," she said as she stared at the picture.

Nash wrapped an arm around her midsection and held her close. He closed his eyes a moment as he kept his chin lightly on top of her head. He wanted to feel this moment. He suddenly hoped that there were more moments like this with Chastity to come.

As they moved on to the other paintings and pictures, Nash placed his hand under Chastity's hair and against the back of her neck. He stroked his thumb back and forth over her nape. She accepted his need to hold her like this. One look at Riker, and his brother appeared happy.

* * * *

They decided to grab some lunch together before heading home. Riker and Nash were able to get a private table on the balcony looking over the large gardens at an expensive restaurant down the street from the exhibit. There was a bright red umbrella blocking the sun and a sheer curtain that kept the bugs at bay and also gave them some privacy. The waiter took their orders then returned with drinks. Chastity looked out toward the gardens and the warm summer day.

"Penny for your thoughts," Nash said to her, and she turned to him and smiled.

"I've never been here before. It's beautiful, and the view is amazing."

Riker took a sip of his red wine, and then Nash clasped his hands on the table.

"I'm surprised," Nash said.

"Why?" she asked then took a sip from her glass of red wine and placed it back down onto the white linen tablecloth.

"A beautiful woman like you should dine at the finest restaurants in the city with the best views."

She swallowed hard and then traced the rim of her wine glass with her index finger. "I didn't say that I haven't dined at such a fine restaurant, just not this one."

"Did Desi bring you to places like this?" Riker asked, shocking her. Her finger paused on the glass, as she thought about his question. She locked gazes with him. Riker and Nash were big men, and they sat only inches away from her on either side. She wanted more space. She felt herself begin to panic.

Riker held her gaze, and it was a serious expression on his face. "Tell us about him."

"No," she replied without hesitation.

Nash scooted his seat closer. His knee was touching hers, and the small connection caused an instant shock to her system.

"Please." She lowered her eyes to the glass.

Then she felt Nash's hand on her knee. He caressed her skin, and whispered to her. "We want to understand what's going on. We care about you. We don't want you to be in danger."

She snapped her head toward him. "Why do you care?"

Nash looked away from her a moment. She felt Riker scoot closer to her now, too.

She waited, anticipating something but unsure what. Then Nash spoke.

"We lost someone."

She could hear the sadness in his voice. The woman who helped to name the club The Jewelry Box? Now her own heart ached and became filled with emotions she wasn't accustomed to, like jealousy. This woman hurt them, or they hurt her. *God, please don't tell me that they hurt her.*

"The one who helped name The Jewelry Box?" she asked, and Nash nodded. She looked at Riker. He didn't seem as upset as Nash.

"You loved her, too?" she found herself asking, and immediately Riker shook his head in denial.

"We both cared for her. We shared something special. When Maggie died, we were both devastated. She was our lover," Riker explained.

Chastity took a deep, unsteady breath. "How did she die? When?"

"We killed her. It happened two years ago." Nash leaned back to take a sip of his wine.

"What do you mean killed her? Please explain that to me."

"We weren't always in the club business. We made our money in investments, and we used to be federal agents," Riker explained. She was surprised, but also impressed.

"She came into our lives two and a half years ago. About a year into an investigation, we met Maggie, and things just happened between the three of us. As the investigation began to get intense, we were about to expose the mastermind behind a huge international drug smuggling operation. We became marked men, and the bad guys blew up our boat. Maggie was supposed to meet us there. She had called and told us she was waiting, with a surprise. On our way there, we were tipped off about a deal going down, and we called Maggie to tell her we would be late but she didn't answer. We got concerned, and then we both got calls threatening us. They said that they would go after our girlfriend. Of course we rushed to the marina, with backup, and as we got there, we saw Maggie waving to us," Riker explained.

"She looked right at us as she stood on the boat. We were fifteen minutes late." Nash ran his hand over his face.

"The boat exploded as we ran down the dock toward her. We didn't make it in time. Someone set a bomb," Riker said.

Chastity reached for Nash's hand and for Riker's.

"I'm so sorry. I can't believe that you had to go through that. Did you ever find out who did it?"

"No," Nash said then brought her fingers to his lips and kissed them.

"This is why we want to make sure that you're not in any danger. Who is this guy, Chastity?" Riker asked her.

She closed her eyes, took a deep breath, and began to explain.

"So you don't know much about him? Not even where he just left for business?" Nash asked.

"No. Every time I asked him questions, he would tell me that he inherited his money and that he did odd jobs now, just to keep busy. I asked him what kind of odd jobs and he would say importing and exporting."

Nash and Riker looked at one another.

"Any distinguishing tattoos on his body?" Riker asked.

"What?" she replied, caught off guard at the question.

"Sorry. So why did you break things off with him?" Nash asked.

"Well, he was getting controlling. He sometimes drank a lot and would be aggressive. But ultimately..." She took a sip of wine, swallowed hard, feeling embarrassed, or as if she weren't good enough. Then Riker caressed her thigh, under the table.

She looked at him and then Nash.

"Ultimately?" Nash asked.

"I caught him in bed with another woman."

"Asshole," Riker stated.

"Numb nuts," Nash added, and she laughed, but felt the sting of tears in her eyes.

"Hey, don't shed a tear for that guy." Nash reached over and caressed his knuckles against her cheek.

"I'm not. It's just that my entire life I've been surrounded by bad situations. No matter how hard I work at getting away from those situations or achieving things, I wind up feeling inadequate or like a failure."

"A failure? How could that be? You're amazing at what you do. That's a success, proven by those you have assisted in business," Riker stated.

"Do you mean a failure in regards to connecting to the right people? To opening up your heart to someone trustworthy?" Nash asked. She nodded her head. He got it. He understood.

Nash curled his finger at her, as he leaned closer across the table. She slowly met him, and when their lips touched, she closed her eyes and felt her heart soar. It was a short, sweet kiss, filled with promise. As he leaned back, Riker cleared his throat. She looked at him and smiled.

"Give me some of that," he whispered and then reached for her. He cupped her head as she leaned closer and they kissed. He gave her hair a little tug, and her pussy reacted immediately. Both of these men were very dominant in nature and obviously resourceful. As she leaned back after Riker's kiss, she couldn't help but admire them. Plus, they used to be federal agents. That was pretty damn sexy.

"Your food has arrived." They looked up toward the waiter and then leaned back in their chairs as the food was delivered. Lobster tails and a small filet sat on each of their plates. It smelled delicious, and soon they were eating, talking about work, their expectations for tomorrow night, and plans for the weekend to spend together.

She smiled, and wondered if this could really work out between the three of them, or would their pasts and hers get in the way?

Chapter 9

Chastity could tell that Nash and Riker, as well as their staff, were nervous. She called them together for a bit of a pep talk, along with Colt.

Standing in the middle of the dance floor, Chastity smiled as thirty employees stood waiting for encouragement.

She clasped her hands in front of her sequined blue dress and smiled toward Riker and Nash. They looked so incredible in their designer dress pants. Nash wore a burgundy button-down dress shirt, and Riker wore a black one. The lights illuminated the club in a gentle glow, and she had yet to tell them that due to her phone calls and contacts they would instantly meet capacity tonight.

"Well, here were are, ladies and gentleman. Opening night for Hidden Treasures, the new hot spot in town. Everyone's contact systems are working, so you are never alone. Just a click on the button."

She tapped Lou's waist and the device clipped on his hip. It was a cross between a phone and a walkie-talkie. It was just like Flynn and Jett's.

"This is a new classy establishment. As long as everyone fulfills the requirements of their jobs and aids your fellow employees in need, you'll be just fine. It has been a pleasure working with all of you and getting to know the two wonderful men behind Hidden Treasures." She glanced at her watch.

"We have four minutes until we open those doors. There is a waiting crowd, so that means instant orders and immediately catering to the customers. Riker, Nash, any words for your staff?" She looked at them.

"We're a team, and we're in this together. Let's be safe, let's have fun, and let's make it worth it all," Nash stated.

"I'm ready," Riker added.

"Man your stations, ladies and gentleman. Tonight, you all put Hidden Treasures on the map," Colton said and they all cheered, then hurried to their stations.

Chastity moved toward Nash and fixed his mic and set on his hip. She did the same for Riker, and then they both took one of her wrists.

She paused as she looked up at them.

"You're amazing, and thank you," Nash whispered.

She smiled. "Everything is going to be great." She hugged them both at the same time. They hugged her back, and then the doors opened.

* * * *

Nash and Riker stood in the office upstairs at the end of the evening. Lou was securing the doors and locking up. They had called down to Chastity, who stayed the entire night and even helped out when things got a little screwed up in the kitchen and in the serving booths.

They couldn't have wished for a more successful night. The compliments were humbling, and Chastity was a total class act. They knew she went above and beyond her call of duty. They watched her smooth over potential situations, and they also saw men flirting with her and passing her their numbers. She handled it with finesse and charm.

Which only made them want her even more. They didn't want to lose her to some other guy, and tonight they needed to act on their feelings and admiration. Tonight, Chastity would be their woman.

Riker heard the knock on the door and opened it. Chastity stepped inside and looked concerned.

"Is everything okay? Did something go wrong?" she asked.

Nash popped the champagne bottle open, making Chastity jump. She covered her heart with her hand and then smiled as Nash poured three glasses.

Nash handed her one, then Riker a glass, too.

"To rebirths and new beginnings," Nash said, and they clicked the three glasses together.

"What a night," she said, and Nash pulled her into his arms as Riker took her glass from her. He kissed her deeply, and she kissed him back. It was an intense moment filled with near desperation. He wanted her so badly he couldn't wait any longer to have her. He forgot about taking it slow and easing into a conversation, touching, feeling, and foreplay. He wanted inside of her, making love to her and sealing their connection.

Chastity kissed him back, and when he pulled from her lips, they were both breathing heavy.

"Chastity, I want you. We want you," Nash stated.

"Just kiss me. Don't talk, don't let me think about all the things that could go wrong. I want you both, too. This is crazy."

He pulled her against him and kissed her again. They fought for control of the kiss while Riker unzipped her dress. The sound of the zipper moving down the sequined dress filled the air.

Nash pulled back and the dress fell to the floor.

There she stood. Their Chastity, the woman they had grown to adore and appreciate, in only a pair of white lace thong panties and no bra.

"Holy Christ, woman, you're gorgeous," Riker said as he reached for her hand, brought it to his lips, and kissed her fingers. Nash watched the intensity in his brother's eyes as he stared into Chastity's and then at her breasts.

Nash pulled off his shirt and undid his pants, and Chastity gasped.

"I don't like underwear," he teased and then pulled her against him. When their skin touched, he nearly moaned from the physical contact. He wanted to touch her everywhere. The feel of her creamy skin under the palms of his hands was invigorating. Nash loved the feel of her curves, of her hips, her lower thighs and her ass. He stroked a finger along the crack then pressed her hard against his body.

Nash felt wild and out of control. Riker undressed and whispered about how beautiful and sexy their woman was.

"You look so sexy wearing the high heels and only a thong, baby. The things I want to do to you," Riker whispered against her neck then grasped her hair.

Nash felt his twin's excitement. He shared the same desire to taste, lick, and suck every inch of this woman before them.

"Tell us you want us both." Nash spoke against her lips.

"Yes. Oh God, yes, Nash. I want you and Riker. Please. Now."

Riker smiled at Nash over Chastity's shoulder.

"Let's take our woman to bed. I want to spread her out and memorize every inch of this perfect body." He caressed his hands down her curves, then back up again, cupping her breasts. The sight of them rising and slowly lowering at Riker's touch aroused Nash.

Nash lifted her up and she immediately straddled his waist. She ran her hands through his hair. He licked a nipple, and she rubbed her breasts against his mouth while pressing her wet cunt against his skin.

She was aroused and ready.

* * * *

Chastity was on fire. She couldn't believe that they wanted her like this. Although, all night she could think of nothing more than kissing them again and spending time with them. Now, here she was, getting ready to make love to Riker and Nash, and she wanted it. She wanted them. She felt so connected to them.

Nash gently laid her on the bed in the back room. She knew they had bedrooms in the back hallway, past the office. They had multiple rooms, practically a home here.

Both men moved into position on either side of her on the bed.

They leaned on an elbow, and simultaneously placed a hand on her belly.

She looked up and tried to make eye contact with both of them, but their simultaneous touch aroused her, and she closed her eyes.

Together, they explored her body. At once, two palms caressed her breasts. They each cupped a mound in their hand as they kissed each shoulder.

"You're incredible, Chastity. So modest and conservative. I knew you had big breasts, but these, these are—" Riker whispered then sucked a nipple into his mouth before he completed his sentence. Nash did the same to her other breast, while cupping it.

When they had their fill of arousing her bosom and making her nipples hard as pebbles, they moved their hands in sync, down her ribs, over her belly, and underneath the small thin straps of her thong panties.

The feel of their hard, thick, masculine hands applying pressure to her sensitive flesh stimulated her senses. She slowly pushed upward, wanting to feel more of their touch.

"Your skin is soft and silky," Nash whispered, and she opened her eyes in time to both see and feel them slowly remove her panties.

She lifted her rear, helping them, and then Riker lifted her panties to his nostrils and inhaled. He closed his eyes, and she watched him, both feeling excited that he wanted to do such a thing and intimidated by his obvious experience with seduction.

She shyly turned her head.

"I think Chastity is embarrassed by your show of desire for her," Nash said and then trailed his fingers along her inner thighs without touching her pussy.

"Oh, please, Nash."

"Are you embarrassed because I like the smell of your pussy on your panties?" Riker asked then leaned down and licked her lower lip.

"Oh God. I am so inexperienced."

"Good," they both stated in sync and rather deeply.

Riker moved his hand down her thigh now, too, after releasing her panties behind him.

She felt their fingers glide up and down her inner thighs. It was torture and she was ticklish. "Please, touch me. I can't take it."

"You mean like this." Nash stroked a finger up and down her moist slit.

"Yes," she replied.

"Or like this?" Riker trailed his finger up and down her slit. They continued to take turns, and it was turning her into a wild woman.

"Stop teasing me. Please stop teasing me." She moved her head side to side.

Stroke, thrust, stroke, thrust.

They continued to stroke her slit, and then thrust fingers into her cunt. When one of them pulled out, the other pushed in. Soon she was panting, lifting her torso up and down on the bed. She couldn't take it. She felt her belly tighten and her core ache with need.

Then both men pulled a nipple into their mouths and she exploded in her first orgasm of the night.

"Fucking beautiful," Riker whispered then kissed her mouth. Once again, he stroked her pussy.

"This is torture," she told him.

"Of the best kind," Riker added.

"We want to take our time, Chastity. We want you to remember our first time together, forever," Nash said then pressed his fingers into her pussy. He thrust them in and out while Riker took her hand and placed it on his cock.

She jumped from the feel of hard, male flesh against her palm. Riker was big and so was Nash.

Something came over her.

"I want to taste you," she told Riker. He smiled and then moved up closer to her mouth. He adjusted her head with a pillow, and she opened her mouth for him.

Slowly, he eased his cock between her lips, and Chastity got her first taste of Riker.

As she got used to a steady pace of sucking him down, Nash pressed a finger to her puckered hole, and she released Riker's cock.

"Whoa! What happened?" Riker asked.

She grabbed a hold of Nash's wrist. "Nash, please. I'm scared of that."

He leaned over her and stared down into her eyes as he stroked her pussy with his fingers.

"You don't like anal sex?" he asked.

"Oh, so that's what nearly shot her off the bed," Riker teased then leaned back down and began to caress her breast again.

"I never did that before."

Nash smiled, and then brushed his lips gently over hers once, twice, three times, before he plunged his tongue deeply.

He kissed her as he maneuvered between her thighs, spreading them wider.

When he released her lips, she felt the tip of his cock against her inner thigh.

"Are you on birth control?" She nodded her head. "Good. Because I don't ever want anything between us."

He pulled back. He aligned his cock with her pussy, and then he leaned one hand down over her shoulder, where he cupped her cheek and neck, causing her to remain focused on him.

"Nice and easy, Chastity. You're made for us," he said and then slowly penetrated her.

Chastity moaned. She felt so tight, and Nash felt too thick, too hard to enter her.

"Oh God, Nash, you're so big."

"And you're so fucking tight, baby. Hold on to me." He leaned down and kissed her lips. She grabbed onto his shoulders and he thrust the rest of the way into her.

She felt his cock to her womb and gasped for a breath. He pulled out then thrust back into her again. When he cupped her face between his hands and stared down into her eyes, she was lost in Nash.

He used his powerful hips to stroke her pussy, over and over again.

"Gorgeous," Riker added, and she moaned again, and again. She felt her body tighten and knew she was going to lose it.

"Nash, I'm coming."

"Me, too, baby. Just a few seconds more." He thrust in and out of her, hard and fast. His hips ground against her hips, their bodies clung together in perspiration and he came, just as she did. They both moaned, then hugged one another close.

Nash kissed her lips, her cheeks and neck, then back to her lips again.

"You're perfect, Chastity. Perfect. I promise to hold out longer the next time. You just feel so fucking good, baby."

She smiled against his mouth and hugged him back. Making love to Nash had been amazing, and she looked forward to doing it again.

* * * *

Riker watched Nash move from the bed to go get washed up in the bathroom. Riker couldn't wait as he lay over Chastity's body and cupped her face between his hands.

He stared into her eyes, and a wave of emotion like nothing before hit him. "I adore you."

She smiled softly, and he felt her fingers trail up and down his back. He maneuvered between her thighs, and she wrapped her legs around his waist. Her pussy was wet and ready for him, but he wanted her to know how deeply he felt for her.

"Seriously, Chastity, I've never felt like this before. I've never told a woman that I adored her."

She leaned up and kissed his upper lip. "I'm glad, and no one has ever told me that they adore me," she added. He smiled, but then thoughts of someone else loving her and touching her brought on waves of fear and desperation. He gripped her hair and head gently between the palms of his hands then kissed her hard on the mouth.

In a flash, it became a game of who could kiss more deeply, and give as good as they were getting.

The feel of her fingers running through his hair encouraged his next move. He adjusted his cock, pulled back, and then thrust forward into her waiting pussy. She gasped, as she released his lips, tilted her head back, but then began to suck on his neck and scratch her nails across his shoulders.

"I love that. You're fucking wild, aren't you, Chastity? You like it dirty."

"Yes. With you, I like it," she said, and he pulled back then thrust back into her. He increased his speed and grabbed a hold of whatever parts of her he could. He massaged, he caressed, and he gripped her body. Then he grabbed a hold of her hips as he lifted up and thrust down into her deeply. Chastity placed her thighs over his thighs, opening up her cunt for a deeper stroke.

"Yes. Deeper, harder, Riker," she cheered him on.

Her breasts bounced and swayed, her cunt leaked and lubricated each stroke, and he lowered over her.

Riker used one hand to cup her ass and thrust into her. She spread wider and lowered her pelvis to let him get deeper. He reached under her, stroking into her, making the bed moan and the headboard bang.

"Fuck, Chastity, you got me there."

"Me, too. Oh God, me, too, Riker." She moaned against his shoulder, and he used the cream from her pussy to stroke over her anus. She was sopping wet, and his dick was ready to burst.

"Mine. I adore you, Chastity. You drive me wild." He pressed his finger against the puckered hole, making her buck beneath him. He thrust the digit in and out of her ass, in sync to his cock's strokes into her pussy. He didn't know how he did it. He didn't know where he got the strength and energy from, but he dug deep.

Chastity screamed and shook beneath him, and then he roared, sucking into her neck and shoulder, as he pulled his finger from her ass. He rolled her to the side, keeping her snug against his chest, and his cock still implanted deep inside of her.

"Amazing," Nash said then joined them on the bed with a washcloth for Chastity and a high five for Riker.

Chapter 10

"Say that again, Luke," Desi stated as they sat in the limo on the way back home from the airport.

"I thought you knew where those two assholes were this whole time."

"Luke, what the fuck are you talking about? Karen never texted me the name of this guy who was hitting on Chastity. I think she was pissed because I wasn't around for her to come over for some action."

"You said that Karen was at a place called Hidden Treasures?"

"Yeah, some new place on the West Side, I think. I really don't care. One of the two guys wants her and I'm not going to let him have her."

Luke was looking at a magazine and then back up at Desi.

"What?"

"I don't know how to tell you this. I fucking don't believe this."

"What? What? Spit it the fuck out already." Desi raised his voice, and Luke turned the magazine around to show him.

"The owners of the club are Nash and Riker Riley. Chastity's been working with them this past month."

Desi felt his blood pressure rising. He stared at Luke.

"They're dead. They're not taking Chastity from me."

"Fuck, Desi, you've got to get this under control. You have to get Chastity back or just forget about her."

"What are you talking about?"

Luke whispered to Desi so that the driver of the limo wouldn't hear him. "If you don't get her away from them, and they tell her about Maggie, and then you start interfering in her life, they're going to investigate you."

"So what? I don't have a fucking record."

"Your name was on the lease for Maggie's apartment. They were federal agents, and if they dig deep enough, or have you followed, then what? Jose will fucking freak if this situation blows the whole operation."

"Son of a bitch." Desi ran his fingers through his hair. "Fuck, I can't believe that this is happening. What are the fucking chances of this happening? I can't give her up." He leaned back and placed his fingers under his chin. He thought about what he could do, and then he looked at Luke.

"What if I threaten to kill them? What if I scare Chastity so much that she breaks up with them?"

"Then you're giving up info on yourself that could be used against you later. I say, cut your losses and forget the bitch. She wasn't even good in bed."

"Says fucking who?"

"You. If she was, then you wouldn't have strayed."

"Fuck you."

"No, fuck you. You need to get out of this, or you're going to wind up having to knock off two retired agents, and Chastity as well."

* * * *

Chastity headed home after work. She couldn't believe it. Friday night had been the best night of her entire life. She made love with Riker and Nash multiple times into Saturday morning. Sunday had been spent all day in Nash's and Riker's arms at their penthouse, where they cooked dinner together and talked about their lives. It was so wild, and she still couldn't quite get her head around the fact that she was dating two men. She was in a ménage relationship, and proud of it.

Even though only a week had passed, it felt as if she had known Riker and Nash forever. How cliché was that?

After she took a quick shower then dried her hair, she placed the dress onto the bed. She would wear this dress this evening. She was going to be meeting them at Hidden Treasures. The best news she had gotten all day was an announcement in the newspaper by a reviewer for an elite New York magazine. They gave the highest rating of five stars to Hidden Treasures, plus wrote up a small article about the place, calling it a treasure of its own, right here, on the West Side of Manhattan.

She sent two copies of the magazine, with the article bookmarked and a small figurine of a mermaid to Riker and Nash. They should be getting it by the time she headed out to the club.

Smiling to herself, she pulled on the dress, fixed her makeup, then grabbed an overnight bag and her purse. She'd already called a taxi, since Riker and Nash would bring her home tomorrow.

She opened her door and gasped. There was Desi.

Her emotions changed from excited to scared shitless in a heartbeat. Her stomach instantly ached, and she couldn't even find her voice. Desi stared at her with evil in his eyes.

He was a big man and towered over her. The expression on his face was one of satisfaction and trouble.

He closed the door, and she walked backward.

"Where are you going all dolled up?"

"Why are you here? Get out, Desi. I don't have anything to say to you."

He took a step toward her. "I have a lot to say to you."

She stared at him. She wouldn't be able to fight him off if Desi attacked her. Not that he ever hit her, but he was a beast in the strength department. She needed to try a different tactic. She needed to remain calm.

"Why don't we get together another time? I'm late for an appointment."

"With those two assholes from the club?" he asked.

"What?"

"Don't 'what' me, Chastity!" he yelled, causing her to jump and drop the bags she held. Her cell phone fell onto the rug, and she stared at it a moment then back at Desi.

"The two men you're fucking. I know them. I know who they are and where they live."

She shook her head as fear filled her insides. What would he do to them? Could he hurt Nash and Riker?

"Why? Why are you doing this to me? You know it wasn't working between us."

"They'll use you, treat you like their sex whore then kill you."

"No. You don't know what you're talking about. You have no right to speak to me like this." She raised her voice and the slap across her cheek came out of nowhere.

She yelped as the pain radiated along her jaw. She tripped over her bags, trying to get away from him.

"They're no good. They'll destroy you and hurt you. You don't belong with them. You belong with me. They'll kill you as if you're meaningless, just like they did to her." He grabbed her by the front of her dress. The material ripped and she screamed then slapped her hands at his hands.

He backhanded her again then grabbed her face and screamed at her. "You will leave them. You will call it off and end it, or I will end them. You hear me, Chastity? I will kill them. I swear, I'll kill them, and show you their fucking heads. Do you want that?" He continued to yell as she cried and shook her head. "Please don't hurt them. Please."

He shook her hard, then he shoved her against the door. Her head hit the metal door, and she thought she actually saw stars. What had he said about Nash and Riker killing a woman? Did he mean Maggie? How would Desi know about that?

Desi grabbed her face between his hands and pressed his body against hers. Her dress was ripped. Her shoulder and part of her bra and breast were visible to him. He looked her over.

"You will do this, Chastity. You end it with them. You end it tonight."

He kissed her brutally hard on the mouth. He thrust his hips against her, hard, causing her spine to hit the door. It hurt so badly, and she prayed he wouldn't force himself on her. He cupped her breast and ripped the dress, scratching her shoulder as he pulled his mouth from hers.

She spit at him. The anger and disgust at his treatment of her was overwhelming.

This was how her mother spent her last days of her life. Under the thumb of an abusive batterer and ex-lover—a victim of domestic violence.

He grabbed her chin and mouth, squeezing so hard that she knew there would be bruises.

"I will hurt you so badly, Chastity. If you push me far enough, I'll make you watch while I kill your two lovers, slowly. That's what I should have done to them when they killed her."

"When they killed who?"

He shoved her head back against the door. "I knew Maggie. Did they tell you about her?" he asked.

Her eyes widened, instantly giving away that she had heard about Maggie.

"She loved them, and they used her."

"There was a bomb on the boat."

He shoved his knee against her thigh. She cried out. "They knew that the bomb was there. They wanted to catch the men who set them up. They chose to go after them and a case, instead of getting Maggie off the boat. They killed her. They caused her death, and they'll cause yours."

"No. No, you're lying."

He shoved his forearm against her throat. She grabbed onto his forearm to try and pry it off of her.

"You better not tell them a damn thing. I will hunt them and you down, and I will kill all three of you. But you'll watch me kill Nash and Riker. You'll listen to their pleas of mercy, and you'll wish you were deaf. I'm giving you one last chance, Chastity. You either come with me when I return for you or watch those scumbags die."

He shoved her to the side and smacked her in the back of the head. She fell to the floor crying and gasping for air as the emotions and the fear rocked her body.

She heard the door slam closed, and when she looked up, he was gone.

Chastity reached for her cell phone. She wasn't sure who to call. She wouldn't call Nash and Riker. She wouldn't get them killed. Desi was crazy. She could call the police. Desi violated the order of protection, but what good had that done her? It was more like an order of illusion. Not even that could stop Desi from assaulting her.

She thought about calling Adelina, but she would tell Flynn and Jett. So would the detectives if she called them.

What about Colt? Colt will do what I ask of him. Colt can help me.

* * * *

Colt was shaking, he was so angry. He was pissed off at Desi and upset with Chastity for refusing to call the police, Nash, or Riker.

He used his key to unlock the door and nearly had a heart attack at the sight. The place was a mess. A broken lamp on the floor by the door. Blood on the rug, and Chastity, curled up in a ball, shaking.

"Oh Jesus, baby. Oh God, that son of a bitch. I'll kill him. Fuck." He fell to his knees and reached for her, but her hair was covering her face.

"Oh God, Colt. I hurt everywhere," she cried.

He slowly pushed her hair from her face, and anger filled him to his core. He clenched his teeth and stared at her in shock.

"Is it bad? I didn't want to look, and then everything started throbbing."

He saw her shoulder, the gash and the blood oozing from there. Her cheek and eyes were swollen and black and blue. Her dress was ripped, and he feared that Desi had done worse. He pulled out his cell phone.

"Yes, I need an ambulance. A woman's been assaulted, and she had an order of protection."

"Colt, no! No, Colt, no police, no ambulance. Hang up the phone!" she yelled at him, her body shaking.

He hung up the phone and caressed her hair, as he held her gaze. The tears rolled down her cheeks. She was a mess, and this was unacceptable. Whatever she was afraid of, they would deal with it together.

"You cannot live in fear like this, Chastity. You cannot allow this monster to get away with this. It doesn't matter what his threats were, or what he told you to make you so scared that you're not even willing to seek medical treatment. It ends here. You are not alone."

He listened as Chastity sobbed, and her words were mumbled between gasps and cries. "He's going to kill them if I don't leave them. He's going to kill Nash and Riker. I can't let that happen."

* * * *

The entire crew was waiting in the visitor's room. Cash, Zane, Hudson, Jagger, Emerson, Stone, Jett, Flynn, and Adelina. Nash and Riker were talking to the detectives who informed him that Desi was nowhere to be found. But then they had informed him they couldn't do a thing if Chastity didn't press charges.

"She's scared. This son of a bitch scared her so much that she didn't even want to get medical treatment," Colt told them. Nash looked at Colt. He had blood on his shirt. Chastity's blood. He had a horrible feeling inside, and he wondered how this could happen.

"We really need to talk with Chastity. We need to find out exactly what he threatened her with. That may help us to find out more about this shithead," Cash said to them. They were all talking about it, and planning security for her, and for Nash and Riker.

"Colt Morgan?" The doctor emerged with a clipboard in hand.

"Yes, that's me."

"Miss Malone placed your name down as family. I would like to go over her injuries with you."

"Yes, of course. But these are all her friends, and these men are her—"

"I'm her boyfriend," Nash stated.

"I'm sorry, sir, but she didn't place your name down on this list. Just Mr. Morgan's."

"Bullshit. What room is she in?" Riker asked.

"Calm down, Riker. She's upset, and she's been threatened. She's obviously scared," Stone said as he placed his hand on Riker's shoulder.

"I don't know what's going on here, but Miss Morgan was very distraught and has numerous bruises. We had to sedate her, to calm her down. She'll be spending the night," he stated.

"Doctor, Miss Malone is involved in a domestic violence situation. Her life was threatened as well as her boyfriends' lives. This is the detective in charge of the case, and myself, and my partner Zane Heston are involved as well. She's scared, and the worst thing we could do right now is waste time. She has information that will help capture the man responsible for her injuries," Cash Corbin stated. The doctor seemed to think about it a moment.

"There are rules for a reason. However, I cannot stand in the way of an investigation." Cash nodded his head and thanked him. The doctor grabbed Cash's arm. "She's distraught. I mean terrified and she needs comfort, not demands and yelling." The doctor gave a stern expression toward Riker.

Riker lowered his head. "I'm sorry, Doc. I'm in love with the woman, and she was just assaulted by some monster. I'm trying my hardest here," Riker admitted then realized what he said and looked at Nash. Nash placed his hand on Riker's shoulder. "I'm in love with her, too. We'll get through to her."

The doctor cleared his throat. "I get it now. Why don't the three of you go in to see her. She may fall asleep as the sedative kicks in."

"Thank you, Doc," Nash said. Nash, Riker, and Colt followed the doctor out of the room. Their buddies each touched their arms or shoulders in support.

* * * *

Nash felt his throat tighten up and tears fill his eyes. Chastity was all bruised and battered. Her eye was swollen shut, her cheek black and blue, and her chin was, too, and even her neck had bruises. There was a big bandage on her shoulder, and she was lying on her side. From where he entered the room, he could see more bandages down her back. He glanced at Riker, who ran his fingers through his own hair and shook his head.

"Oh God."

"Colt?" Chastity whispered in a groggy voice.

"Yeah, baby, it's me. How are you doing now?" He leaned over and gently pushed strands of hair away from her face.

"I want to go home, Colt. I'm not safe here. Bring me to your place," she whispered, and her voice sounded like it clogged up with tears.

"Baby, you need protection. The kind of protection that my place doesn't have."

"No. Please, Colt."

Colt looked at Nash and Riker with pleading eyes. Nash could see the tears in Colt's eyes. He loved Chastity. They really were best friends.

"Chastity?" Riker whispered, and she turned suddenly toward him. She blinked her eyes, and then shook her head. She turned her face into the pillow.

"Go away, Riker. Please just leave and forget about me."

Riker moved to where Colt was, and Nash joined him. Nash placed his hand on her hip. Riker leaned down, and somehow had the composure to not lose it, seeing her bruises.

"Baby, we love you. We're going to protect you," Riker whispered.

Tears rolled down her cheeks. "You can't protect me. He's going to kill both of you."

"No, baby, he can't get to us. We know who he is now. The police are looking for him, and the detectives."

"No, Nash. Stop them. He'll kill both of you. He knows where you live, and who you both are."

Her words were mumbled. The sedatives were slowing down her speech, but she was trying so hard to talk.

"So what. It doesn't matter. We were agents, remember? We've dealt with worse individuals than this guy," Riker said then smiled as he caressed the hair from her face.

"You don't understand," she started to say, and then her eyes began to roll back.

"Rest, Chastity. Rest and we'll talk about it tomorrow, when you're feeling better," Nash said.

"He knows you…both. He knew…Maggie," she whispered then fell asleep.

Chapter 11

Their friends remained in the waiting area. Nash and Riker stormed out of Chastity's room and into the crowd of their best friends. Colt remained behind with Chastity.

Riker knew that he needed to calm down and gain some control here. Nash wanted to go all John Wayne on the situation, and rightfully so.

"What is it? What the fuck happened?" Cash asked as Zane and the others walked closer.

Everyone they trusted was in this room. The expressions of concern gave Riker confidence that with their help, they could keep Chastity safe.

"We've got ourselves a hell of a problem," Riker stated.

"The motherfuckers that killed Maggie have a hand in this. Fucking Desi may be one of them," Nash stated.

"Holy shit," Emerson said.

"My God, how the hell?" Cash began to say.

"It doesn't fucking matter, Cash," Riker said.

"What matters is that we need to find this asshole pronto. Nash and I need to set up a command center and a safe place for Chastity. It can't be at our place or the club."

"Okay. We'll figure this out. Are you going to call the agency?" Zane asked.

Riker looked at Nash.

"We'll inform our ex-commander, but we're not keeping out of the loop. This son of a bitch is going down, and so is the operation that we never were able to destroy," Nash said, and they all nodded in agreement.

"We've got your backs. We're right here with you," Jett stated.

Nash and Riker locked gazes.

Nash spoke his words through clenched teeth.

"They won't take her away from us. They won't get to her like they did to Maggie."

Chapter 12

It was like being in some spy-type guy flick. Instead of 007, she had 0014. Nash and Riker looked different. Their eyes were dark, their expressions controlled, unemotional, determined, and it both frightened Chastity and aroused her. She tried stopping them from taking her with them. She didn't want them to get killed. They said they found things out about Desi, and about his real job, and real life. They were even angrier.

Flynn and Jett were there, plus their other two friends, Emerson and Stone, who appeared just as lethal and good looking as her own men.

She couldn't stop the shaking. Her body ached, and especially her cheek and shoulder. Nash covered her securely in a blanket. They placed a wig over her head, to disguise her.

"Stone is going to carry you out of here. It's just a precaution. We're going to get into the vehicle downstairs, and then we'll be back together for the rest of our trip. Okay, Chastity?" Riker asked her.

She looked from Riker to Stone. Stone was big and tall like Riker, and he appeared mean, but then he winked at her.

"Oh, I'm going to like this assignment," he whispered, making her smirk.

"He tries to feel you up, you hit him. Don't take any of his crap," Nash stated.

Chastity heard the serious tone in Nash's voice despite the way he gave Stone a nudge.

Riker leaned down to kiss her then secure the wig. "I like you better as my blonde mermaid," he told her. Her belly tightened.

Nash kissed her next. Then he placed his fingers under her chin. "We are always nearby. You'll be out of our sight for sixty-two seconds." He kissed her again before he and Riker left the room.

"Sixty-two seconds?" she whispered.

"They timed it, sweetheart. They're not taking any chances with you," Jett stated, then winked.

"Jett, Flynn, you're sure that Nash and Riker will be safe? You're sure that Desi can't get to them? I'm scared. You weren't there. You don't know what Desi looked like," she whispered as a tear rolled down her cheek.

Stone reached over and gently wiped it away.

Flynn and Jett smiled at her.

"A lot of things have become clear," Flynn stated. "Things they'll discuss with you when we get you to the safe location. But know this, Riker and Nash are good at what they do. They're in agent mode right now, and that's what's going to keep them and you safe. So no worries, okay, beautiful?"

She swallowed hard. "Okay."

"Great. Now this is my part. The absolute best part of the entire mission," Stone teased, rubbing his hands together and licking his lips.

"Cool it, Stone, and get serious," his brother Emerson said as he opened the door to the room and peeked down the hallway.

He raised his thumb, an indication that things were good.

Stone reached for her. "Put your arms around my neck and let me know if anything hurts too much." He raised his eyebrows at her. She had to laugh. He really was quite the character.

As he lifted her into his arms, she felt sore, but it was bearable. All she wanted to do was to get to Riker and Nash, and to feel them in her arms.

Chastity was carried from her bed in the hospital, down a hallway, a private staircase, and to the basement. There were men standing guard, holding weapons, and whispering into wrist mics. She had no idea how resourceful Riker and Nash were. The men she saw appeared well equipped and alert. It reinforced the seriousness of this situation. She realized that this went beyond a domestic violence situation and couldn't help but to think about Nash and Riker's relationship with that Maggie woman. Who was she? How did Desi know her? What was all of this really about?

"Hold on, darling. We have about ten seconds left to get you to that SUV, or Riker and Nash are going to have our asses," Stone said as the door to the side entrance opened, and there sat the SUV. There were two men in black suits standing next to it. To the right and to the left, she saw others standing guard. Her insides did a series of flips and flops.

She couldn't see inside the door, but right before Stone began to place her inside, he smiled down to her.

"Good luck. Stay safe, and listen to your men." He kissed her on the cheek, and then lifted her into the backseat. Immediately she felt the set of hands lifting her further inside. A quick glance to her left and there was Riker.

"Come on, baby. Everything is going down right on schedule."

The door closed and as Riker adjusted her body on the sheet-covered seats next to him, she saw Nash.

He was looking at his watch, and speaking into a wrist mic. "You were three seconds off, asshole."

She panicked a moment. Was he really that angry with Stone for being three seconds late? Then he laughed, and she sighed in relief.

"You okay, baby? Not too sore?" Riker asked her.

She turned to look at him. "You're sure this is the right thing to do? You and Nash will be safe?"

He stared into her eyes as he placed his hand under her hair and against the back of her head and nape.

"We won't let anything happen to you. Everything has become quite clear to us."

He leaned forward and kissed her softly. Then she heard Nash.

"Lie down and rest, Chastity. I don't want you pushing it and feeling pain," he told her very seriously.

She looked at him and smiled, but he didn't smile back. He seemed different. He seemed guarded and distracted. Was it because of the danger they were in, or did it have something to do with Maggie? She couldn't help but wonder and feel jealous. Was he thinking about Maggie now? Had Maggie really meant that much to Nash and Riker?

She leaned back against Riker as some doubts and reservations about what was to come exploded through her mind. There would be no future with her if they couldn't let go of the past, let go of their thoughts, and let go of their love for Maggie. She couldn't compete with a ghost or fight with them about their loss. It wouldn't be right to give them a hard time because they lost the woman Nash loved, and that he and Riker shared as a lover.

She didn't know what that felt like. All she knew was that she never truly loved until Nash and Riker. If she lost them, or if they were killed, she would want to die, too. Life just wouldn't be worth living.

She felt the tears fill her eyes, and she turned into the leather upholstery to hide her tears and her heavy heart.

* * * *

Riker stared down into Chastity's face as he lifted her sleeping form into his arms. Her face was battered and bruised, and it really pissed him off. He should have been there for her. They knew that her ex wanted her back, and that he was constantly calling. How could they have been so stupid?

He softly kissed her lips, and she moaned in his arms.

He began to carry her, and with each step, she became more alert.

Slowly she moved her arms up and around his shoulders and cuddled her face against his neck. Her softness and her sweet scent calmed him momentarily.

"Cash said that they picked up Luke, Desi's partner. They have men questioning him now," Nash whispered as he spoke into the cell phone.

"Good. Maybe they'll be able to interrogate him and get us more on Desi," Riker replied. He squeezed Chastity a little snugger. The thought that people were out there ready to harm them made him feel on edge.

"I don't recognize these guys securing the building," Nash stated to Riker. Riker was thinking the same thing, but then again, he and Nash had been out of the agency for a couple of years now. There were many new faces.

As they got into the elevator and made their way to an executive penthouse suite of the Four Seasons hotel, Riker couldn't wait to get Chastity inside the room. She would be safe there. He knew that the team would have everything set up in the next room adjacent to theirs. They could remain on top of the investigation, while also personally protecting Chastity.

The door opened, and they exited together. Cash and Zane were there to greet them.

"Glad you made it here okay," Cash said then shook Nash's hand.

"The bedroom is that way, Riker," Zane told him then directed him toward the back area. To the right, Riker could see that the agents and their friends were already set up. There were computers, multiple surveillance devices, and other paraphernalia the federal agents used during a sting operation.

Zane pulled down the covers to the king-sized bed. Riker nodded a thank-you then softly placed Chastity down onto the bed. She was still wearing the wig and only the hospital gown beneath the blanket. She opened her eyes and held on to his forearms.

"Riker?"

"Shh, baby, everything is okay. It's going as planned." He removed the wig, tossing it to Zane, who took it and exited the room.

Riker moved the strands of blonde hair from her face. "I'm not going to let anything happen to you." He held her gaze as a million thoughts and fears exploded in his mind. He was so in love with Chastity. She was everything he and Nash ever wanted in a woman. Maggie never compared. It never felt like this with her. With Chastity was where their love and their hearts belonged.

"I'm scared. I want you to tell me everything."

"Baby, please. Just rest and let us handle it."

"No. No Riker, I want to know. I can tell that Nash is hurting. What is it?"

"Hey, they're setting everything up in the other room. Commander Samone is here, too. They got an update and need us," Nash stated as he approached the bed. Chastity looked at his gun and swallowed hard.

"No worries, okay? We're armed, and it's for your protection and ours," Riker told her.

"Do you want to shower? We got a bunch of clothes for you. Adelina helped Jett and Flynn. We didn't want to take a chance at going to your apartment, then being followed," Nash said. And even Riker thought he sounded distant. He would need to speak with his brother. Chastity was scared enough, and she didn't need his attitude. Nash always got this way when he was on a case. His intensity helped to bring justice and arrest the criminals.

"Yes. A shower would be great," she said.

* * * *

"Okay, the food will be up here soon. You'll have enough time. Riker can help grab some clothes for you. They're in the drawers and the closet.

Nash turned and walked out of the room, and Chastity felt the ache in her heart. He was already pushing her away. He was placing distance between them. Was it because he was thinking about Maggie? She couldn't help but feel jealous and sad.

"Let me help you," Riker said then assisted her off the bed and into the large bathroom.

She didn't reveal the ache she felt. She didn't want him worrying about her. In her head, she feared that this situation would come between the three of them. It would tear them apart, and she needed to keep that possibility in the back of her mind.

"You can leave me. I'll be okay," she told Riker as he helped lift the gown off of her, after starting the water in the shower.

"Oh God, baby. Damn." He looked over her injuries. She was battered and bruised. There were other bruises in places she hadn't even recalled that Desi had caused. Like the one on her inner thigh and leg.

"I'll be okay. Go take care of business."

He kissed her cheek then squeezed her naked body against his. His warm breath caressed her ear. His hands smoothed over her ass and back, and she felt his erection against her belly.

"I love you, baby. I can't wait to hold you in my arms in bed." He kissed her ear and then walked away, closing the door behind him.

Chastity turned toward the mirror and her battered skin. The tears flowed from her eyes, and her heart ached. She loved them both so much. But it seemed like this wouldn't last. Their love wouldn't survive, just like the other things in her life.

She stepped into the shower and cringed at the ache the flowing water caused against her cuts and bruises. She absorbed that pain and accepted it, for nothing was as bad as the pain in her heart. Nothing would be worse than losing the love of Riker and Nash.

* * * *

"Riker, Nash, sit down," Commander Samone told them as they sat in a small sitting area away from the other agents and their friends.

"What is it?" Nash asked.

He could tell that his commander looked grim and angry. "Your friends Cash and Zane found out some interesting information. This man, Desi Merdock, knew Maggie."

"We know that. We just don't know how," Nash stated.

"Cash and Zane found out that her apartment lease was in Desi's name," Samone stated.

"What does that mean?" Riker asked.

"Our agents took it a few steps further. I don't know how to tell you this, Nash. But she was working with Desi. They, along with a guy named Luke Propell, are the heavies for that drug operation you two were working. It seems she was sent in to set you two up."

"No. No fucking way. Where did you get this information?" Nash asked, raising his voice and rising from the chair. He drew everyone's attention.

"As you know, we have Luke in custody. After a bit of questioning, we found out that Maggie was sent to seduce the two of you. She then was told to get you two to the marina, where she helped set up the bomb to kill you. She was supposed to leave the boat. Luke said that their boss had other men set the bomb that exploded as back up, in case Maggie failed. You were both getting too close and were going to figure out the leader of the operation."

Nash couldn't believe what he was hearing. Maggie had used him and Riker? Maggie had lied about her feelings for them? She manipulated them into bed? She seduced them? He had struggled with her death for the last two years. He hadn't fully lived his life out of guilt.

"Nash?" Riker said his name and placed his hand on his shoulder.

Nash pulled away. "I don't fucking believe this."

"I know you're upset. But right now, as we speak, the team is gathering more evidence. We got leads on some locations, and the operation headquarters, Nash. We're within reach of taking down the operation, and the leader that caused all this shit," Commander Samone said.

Nash looked at Riker. He couldn't help the betrayal he felt and the anger toward Maggie and the agency. Now Chastity knew Desi. How?

"Have the agents investigated Chastity?" he asked and felt the bile fill his throat at even thinking she was part of this, never mind saying the words.

"What the fuck are you thinking? You don't really believe that she's involved?" Riker asked this time, raising his voice.

Now their friends joined the conversation.

"No way. There's no way that she's involved," Cash told them.

"How do you know? How do we fucking know?" Nash raised his voice.

"She has no family. She came here from Charlotte to start a new life," Zane told Nash.

"And you know this how? How did she get involved with Colt? How come she doesn't have any family? What if she's involved with this, too? What if she seduced us like Maggie did?"

"You don't believe that, do you, Nash?"

Everyone turned to see Chastity, standing in the doorway. Her hair was wet, and she wore a light green sundress and was barefoot.

Nash felt his gut clench. He feared everything. He felt so confused.

"I don't know what to believe," Nash stated. He turned away and shook his head. He ran his hands through his hair in frustration and confusion. His heart ached. It literally ached.

"Fuck that. You fucking know that she's the real thing. I know you're upset. I know that you feel betrayed. So do I, Nash, but Chastity is not part of this. It's a sick fucking coincidence," Riker told Nash.

"We can't afford to believe in coincidences," Nash said as he held Chastity's gaze.

"Let's just calm down and not jump to conclusions. I'm sure that if we have any questions, Chastity will be more than willing to answer them," the commander stated.

Chastity straightened her shoulders and walked into the room. She now stood directly in front of Nash and Riker.

"You asked me to trust you. You promised to protect me, to love me, and it wasn't easy for me to do. I understand that this woman hurt you. But the fact that you think I am somehow involved with this hurts more than anything. More than Desi's attack and more than the inadequacy I've felt my entire life until meeting both of you. I get it. I see how it is."

She turned toward their commander.

"I'll answer any questions you have, but not with them present. Hook up a lie detector. Do whatever it is you do to ensure that someone is telling the truth. I will do it, and then I'm leaving."

"Chastity, you're not going anywhere," Riker said, but she didn't turn to look at him or Nash. Nash walked out of the room, and Riker followed him. So did the others.

* * * *

Cash sat down next to Chastity. He took her hand into his own, as she tried her hardest not to cry. This was a total nightmare. Just like those in her past who said they loved her had failed her, now so did the two men she loved more than life itself.

"Miss Malone, my name is Commander Samone. I'm the federal agent in charge of the investigation. I have some questions for you, since you are willing to answer them."

She nodded her head at the man. He looked fierce. He had dark hair and a bit of gray by his ears. She pinned him as being in his fifties, and uptight, maybe even paranoid, as he looked her over.

She glanced at Cash.

"I'm staying here with you. No one is charging you with anything. We're just asking questions to verify who is or isn't involved with this."

"Oh, you're wrong, Cash. I've already been accused, charged, and sentenced. It's over between Riker, Nash, and I. I'll cooperate. I have nothing to hide. I can't fight for something, for two people who can't trust me."

She looked toward the commander and asked him to begin.

* * * *

"Let's listen in. I don't believe that she is involved. It's not true and you need to get your head out of your ass, brother," Riker said. They stood in the other room, listening along with their friends and some agents as their commander interrogated their woman.

But she wasn't their woman anymore. She'd told Cash she was done with them. She was right. In a flash, they'd turned against her and believed that she could somehow be involved. Riker knew that she wasn't. He loved her more than anything, and now their past careers as agents were about to take the one woman they truly loved away from them.

They all listened to Chastity answer the questions. Their commander wasn't going easy on her, not by a long shot. But the entire time, Chastity kept her cool, and even asked for a lie detector test, or whatever devices they had, to prove that she was innocent and not involved with the case.

As the commander backtracked about her life in Charlotte, more heartbreaking information came out. Chastity had been through so much in her life.

"So your mother was involved in an abusive relationship?"

"Yes. It went on for over a year, and when she wound up hospitalized after one of his beatings, she left him."

"Where were you at the time?"

"Hiding."

"Hiding from him? Why? Didn't your mother take you with her?" They heard her shaky voice as she revealed information about her past. "He refused to let me leave with her. It was a bad night for both of us."

"How did you get out?"

"I didn't," she whispered.

"How did your mother die?" the commander asked.

"At the hands of another untrusting, abusive man."

"And where were you at the time?"

"I was working and saving money to leave home. I had finished up college and was determined to get out of Charlotte and away from my mother's problems. It's kind of funny, when you think about it."

"How so?" Cash asked.

"I ran as far away as I could go, established myself in a career, and tried to be careful about whom I dated, and I fell for a man who lied and manipulated me, just as my mother's boyfriends had done."

"How did you meet Desi?"

"I met him at one of the restaurants I was working at. It was located near Fulton's Fish Market. A really nice quaint place that just needed their menu and decor tweaked a bit. He came in with a few guys, and I was helping the manager with some of the setup when she knocked some things over. I had to smooth things over with Desi and his friends. He was older, attractive, and seemed very nice. He played me from the start I guess."

"Didn't you ask him what he did for a living? Once you started dating and going out together?" the commander asked.

"He said that he inherited his money. I was innocent and naive, and he was obviously manipulative and conniving. What more do you want to know? Don't you think I felt stupid enough to stay with him, to believe his lies, to give my virginity to the man? It was a mistake. Obviously one I will live with for the rest of my life."

"I don't think he used you, Chastity. I think he actually cares for you. Maybe an obsession, or a need to possess you, but men like this, they don't do commitments," Cash told her.

"Commitments? Men like Desi, like my mother's killer, her exes, take total control of a woman's mind. They get you where you no longer feel like you can live without their assistance, without their permission until you can't breathe. They slowly take the life out of you."

"But you left him. You broke things off," the commander said.

"I snapped out of the fog. I was so fearful that I would end up like my mother, like other women do, that I slowly started pulling back. The more space I forced, the more things I saw. Like his over drinking, and the use of his strength. I could never fight a man like Desi off. Hence my current condition. He gave me an ultimatum the other night. So you may be right, Cash. Maybe Desi really does care for me."

"What was the ultimatum?" the commander asked.

She was silent a moment. "Give up Nash and Riker. Break things off with them, or they would die in front of me, and then I would die, too."

"Jesus," Cash whispered.

The tears rolled down her cheeks, as she clasped her hands on her lap.

"I may not have known or recognized the signs soon enough that indicated Desi was a batterer and a psycho, but I know the man well enough to tell you that he will do what he said. He told me that Maggie set the bombs herself. He said that she was supposed to kill both Nash and Riker, but it got screwed up. He said that Riker and Nash wanted to catch the people setting the bomb and chose their jobs over Maggie. He wants revenge. He wants them dead. You can believe whatever you want about me, but they need protection."

"So you weren't working for Desi? You didn't seduce them to get close so that Desi could kill them?"

"No. I love them more than life itself. That's why I'm going to help you catch Desi."

"What do you mean? How?"

"You're going to let me leave. Desi is going to come after me, and take me away. I'm going to tell him that I broke things off with Riker and Nash, and that they said they only cared about finding the person behind the huge drug operation. He'll believe me, and hopefully, bring me in on what's going on."

"We're not using you," Cash stated firmly, but the commander leaned back into his chair. She could tell that he wanted to catch this guy. He wanted this case solved, and he didn't care how he did it.

Nash knew that they made her feel like nothing had been worth fighting for in her life until now. Until them. But since they didn't believe her anyway, Chastity probably didn't care if she lived or died. She could help end this case and bring them justice and the truth.

"It's not your choice, Cash. I can get Desi out of hiding. Let's stop wasting time and resources. Just let me walk out of here and head to my place. Do whatever it is you agents do. I don't care. But I'm not staying here. I'm not remaining in a place where everyone, including the two men I love, stand there and wonder if I'm really who I say I am, or if I'm lying. I'm not doing it."

* * * *

"This is what you want, Nash? You want the woman we both love to continue to go through such heartache? To give herself up as bait to prove to us that she's the real deal? 'Cause I'm not willing to risk her life. Desi will fucking kill her. She's not lying. I'm telling you that she has nothing to do with Desi and the operation. Let the others figure the shit out, and let's take care of Chastity," Riker stated to his brother, raising his voice.

Nash just stared at Riker, and Riker wanted to shake some sense into him. Hadn't he heard her words? Hadn't he felt her pain?

"What do we have to lose? Our lives? So fucking what. I don't care. None of it matters. Not the club, not our money, nothing matters but Chastity and having her in our lives, in our bed forever."

"You're right. She can't be involved. I'm fucking paranoid. I don't want to believe it. I'm afraid of feeling the pain. Like when Maggie died. But now I've hurt her so badly."

"She isn't Maggie. You heard the facts. Maggie was working us over."

"You knew. You didn't fall for her like I did. You never loved her, Riker. Why?"

Riker was silent a moment. "I don't know. I wanted to because you did. But it wasn't the same. It's not like when we're with Chastity. I'd die for her, Nash. Just like I would die for you."

"I feel the same way. I fucked this up. I was so fucking upset about the news. I felt confused and didn't think before I spoke. I was so fucking angry. All I've been doing the last two years was blaming myself and pushing everyone away. To find out that Maggie lied and used us burns inside. It fucking hurts."

"Losing Chastity and blaming her for something she had nothing to do with will hurt more. I can't lose her. I love her, and so do you. We'll explain it to her. We can't let Desi get to her. This guy hurt her so badly already. He could have killed her, and if he finds out that she's using him so we can catch him—"

"She'll die," Nash finished.

Chapter 13

Chastity was in the bedroom. She pulled off the dress and was going to put on a pair of jeans and a T-shirt. She heard the bedroom door open and gasped as she turned, holding the dress in front of her.

"What are you doing in here?" she asked both Nash and Riker. They both looked pissed off. Well she was pissed off, too.

"What are you doing?" Nash asked her.

"Changing."

"Going somewhere?" he asked, taking a few slow steps toward her. She backed up until her ass hit the desk behind her.

"You're not leaving us. You're not going to be bait," Riker stated from behind Nash.

"Get out. It's none of your concern. I'm not your concern."

Nash walked closer. "That's where you're wrong. You are our concern. You're our woman, our everything, and you're not risking your life."

"You can't tell me what to do. You can't control me, or make me."

"You think we can't. Hell, woman, you don't know what we're capable of," Riker told her, as he looked her body over. Chastity gulped as she clutched the dress to her body. Why did his statement turn her on? Why was she getting aroused when they had hurt her so badly by not trusting her? *Why am I such a glutton for punishment?*

Nash stared down into her eyes. He was only a foot away from her.

"I jumped the gun. I overreacted out of fear and anger. I know that you're not involved. I was hurt by Maggie and finding out what she did and how she manipulated us just pissed me the hell off. I've wasted so much fucking time. Time alone, pushing away anyone who has been important to me or anyone who made me feel at all," Nash told her.

"I'm not Maggie, Nash. I can't fight against a ghost, not against a person who no longer exists."

"I'm not asking you to. I hurt you, and it will never happen again."

"No, Nash. It won't happen again, because we're over."

He pressed her body against the wall, shocking her. He held her face between his hands and whispered next to her lips.

"We're not over, baby. We've only just begun. I fucked up. Can't you forgive me? I'd do anything for you, Chastity. How can I prove to you that I'm sorry and that I do trust you?"

Chastity felt the tears in her eyes, and she felt Nash's sincerity. But she had been fooled before. She had been taken and manipulated by others. What if he was lying?

As if sensing her fear and distrust, Nash lowered to his knees. He held her hips and hugged her to him. She felt his warm breath against her belly.

"Ah shit, Chastity. You got the man on his fucking knees. If the guys saw this now, he would be ruined in the macho male department," Riker stated.

She smirked as her heart instantly lifted with some relief. If they truly didn't love her, would they go to such extents to prove it?

She gripped Nash's hair, forcing him to look up at her. Now the dress was gone, and there she stood in only her panties and bra.

"You listen to me, and you listen good, mister. I love you. I'm not involved with those assholes. I understand why you overreacted and feared that I was involved. But that doesn't let you off the hook. You've got a lot to prove."

Nash smiled at her then kissed her belly. He made his way up her body then covered her lips with his. He kissed her deeply, and her heart soared with relief and love for this man. But he was going to flip out when she told him about the plan she'd made with the commander.

Nash lifted her up against the wall, and she straddled his waist. He kissed her deeply, and they battled for control of it. She felt his large hands against her skin. Then he ripped her panties off of her. She gasped. She was so aroused, so needy for him to be inside of her. He scraped his lips across her mouth to her neck. Gripping his shoulders and pressing her breasts against his chest and neck, she moaned. "Please, Nash. This is crazy."

She felt him undo his pants, push them down, then align his cock with her slick, wet slit.

He locked gazes with her. He pulled her lower lip between his teeth then gently tugged and released. "No, baby, this is crazy. The need, the desire I have for you is so overwhelming sometimes, I lose it. I don't want to hurt you. I know you have bruises, but fuck it, baby, I need inside now."

"Yes, yes, Nash. Now."

He was already pushing the tip of his cock between her wet folds. He shoved into her and they both moaned. He held his thick, hard cock inside of her for a moment as if the move eased the ache, or filled a gap inside of him.

She ran her hands up his head through his hair and held him best she could.

"I'm sorry, baby. I need you. I'm nothing without you," he told her. Were those tears in his eyes? She wasn't certain, but she knew with all her heart that Nash did love her. He pulled out then shoved back into her. She kissed him hard on the mouth while she countered his thrusts. She didn't care about her bruises, the little aches and pains. She cared about fulfilling the need deep within her core that only Nash and Riker could fill. In and out he stroked her cunt. Then he moved in fast, deep strokes until she moaned her release, squeezing him to her. Then he exploded inside of her and held her so tight.

"I love you, baby. I love you so much," he said.

Chastity smiled then kissed him all over his cheeks, which made him chuckle.

Riker cleared his throat, and when they turned, Riker was completely naked. Chastity felt her cheeks warm as she pulled her lower lip between her teeth and admired her other sexy lover. Riker was the naughty one. The man who talked dirty to her and made her think of doing things that thinking alone made her blush and made her pussy weep.

Nash released her to Riker, who grabbed a hold of her ass and squeezed as he devoured her moans by kissing her deeply. He stroked his finger down her backside and slid his finger from her wet pussy to her anus.

Pressing a finger into her ass, she thrust against him, gasping for air. He released her lips as she held on to his shoulders.

He dipped his hips, and aligned his cock with her wet cunt. Riker held her gaze. "You complete me. Inside you everything is always perfect." He said the last words through clenched teeth as he shoved up into her. His cock was so hard she couldn't stop the louder moan.

He pressed his lips against her mouth while he pulled out, then thrust back into her.

"Shh, baby, there is a crowd of men out there, and they would be so jealous knowing that we're in here fucking our woman."

"Oh God, Riker, you're so bad."

He pulled out then thrust back in. "And you feel so good."

In and out he stroked is hard cock into her pussy. His finger found her ass again. He pushed it against her puckered hole, and she held her breath then released a long sigh.

"Feel good, baby?" he whispered while pumping his hips.

"Yes, oh yes. It's outrageous. It burns, yet I feel so needy."

"You're going to have us both real soon."

"When this is all done. When the operation is complete and all the assholes are behind bars, this ass is mine. Nash and I are going to make love to our woman together, and truly seal the deal that we love you, and you're ours."

He pulled his finger from her ass and began a series of long, deep, hard strokes. She gripped his shoulders, tilted her head back, and tried to remain quiet. It was quite difficult to do, but somehow even that turned her on and made her come. She shook against him as her orgasm rocked her body. Riker smiled then got awfully serious as he stroked his cock into her faster then exploded inside of her. He squeezed Chastity against his chest.

When they heard the knock on the door, she jerked, trying to pull away, but Riker didn't let her. Instead he smacked her ass, and whispered some very naughty and sexually stimulating promises into her ear.

Chapter 14

"I don't like this. I don't like this one fucking bit," Nash said as Riker adjusted the wire. It was hidden beneath her blouse. No one could see it, unless they ripped the material open. But, so many agents, plus her men, would guard her.

The agency got wind of the operation Desi was involved in, and now had a location on the distribution center. The leader of it was due to meet Desi there today. Coincidentally, it was down the street from Fulton's Fish Market. Chastity contacted Desi. She told him that she was hiding out and didn't know what to do. She said that Nash and Riker admitted that they didn't stop Maggie from dying and that they really didn't love her, that they just wanted her for sex. She went on to tell him that they broke things off with her, because they didn't want to be harassed by some ex-boyfriend she still loved. Desi bought it all.

Meanwhile, the agents uncovered his location, and she set up to meet Desi at the little restaurant where they first met. It had been her idea, and ultimately upset Nash and Riker. Their friends calmed them down, but she had to end this craziness. She trusted Nash and Riker to keep her safe. They needed to put the past behind them and lock down the drug operation, its leader and affiliates as well as Desi. Luke had been a big help and was offered a plea bargain for information that led to the capture of those involved.

"You be smart and don't try to be a hero. That's our job," Riker told her then smiled before kissing her lips.

"You do exactly what we said. Do not stray from the plan. Talk to him. Lead him to believe what you say is true, and then get him to take you with him to meet the leader. Keep a wall by your back whenever you can," Nash told her. He was so serious as he rechecked her wire for the tenth time. She took his hands and squeezed them.

"I'll be smart, not stupid. I know that you'll protect me."

They had been over the plan so many times, she wondered if she could pull off the emotions needed to do this. She would dig deep. She wanted a future of happiness, not one laced with fear of always looking over their shoulders.

Nash kissed her then fixed her lipstick.

"How do I look?" she asked.

"Edible," Riker stated.

"We heard that. We can hear everything," one of the agents said, and they laughed.

"Good. Then everyone knows that she's ours." Nash kissed her again.

Chastity had to move around to a few different places before reaching the destination. They didn't want to take any chances that she was followed or that the building was being watched. So they utilized some underground exits and subway maintenance exits to leave the Four Seasons hotel.

* * * *

Chastity walked into the little restaurant and was greeted by the manager. She remembered her immediately and even gave her a hug hello.

"What the hell happened to you?" the manager asked.

"I got mugged. It was an experience I won't ever forget," she told her.

"Holy shit. That stuff still happens? Go figure. Well I'm glad you're okay. Take a seat at that corner table. It's nice and private back there."

"Great. I'm meeting someone."

"Nice. Is he hot?"

"You'll see," she said then winked back.

Chastity walked over and sat at the table. The minutes passed, and she wondered if Desi would be a no-show. Had he somehow figured out that this was a setup? She wished she could speak with Nash and Riker.

She was getting antsy after ordering an iced tea and waiting for a while. Then the door opened. Instantly her body began to shake. She hadn't expected such a fearful reaction to the man. He was so damn big and strong. He wore blue jeans and a button-down shirt. He looked normal. That just didn't sit right with Chastity at all.

The manager greeted him, gave him a wink, took his drink order, then walked away. As he bent down to kiss her cheek, she turned from him. It was instinctive.

He reached up, blocking anyone's view of his move and grasped her chin. "Don't you ever pull away from me," he told her. She held his gaze and felt the tears hit her eyes as the sickness filled her belly. This man was a complete monster. How come she hadn't seen it sooner?

His lips touched hers, and she closed her eyes and tried to pretend that it was okay.

Releasing her lips and his hold, he didn't sit across from her, but instead right beside her, where he could block anyone's view of her.

"Couldn't you put on some makeup to hide that shit on your face?" he asked her, and she was shocked.

"You caused the shit," she replied sarcastically, and without thinking. He gripped her thigh under the table. She gasped.

"I'm sorry. Please let go of my leg. I didn't mean it. I'm just confused and upset. Please, Desi. I need you."

He held her gaze. His eyes as dark as night bore into hers.

"I need you, too. Underneath me, in bed, where you belong."

She turned away from him.

He grabbed her hand from her lap and placed it on the table. He clasped their fingers together. His hands were huge, his grip hard, not gentle at all.

"I'm so fucking pissed off at you. You have no fucking idea what I've been going through."

She looked up at him, and remained silent.

"Why did you hide out so long?"

"I had to. I was confused, and so hurt. You hurt me, Desi. They used me. I was so confused, but then I thought about all the things you told me. You were right. You were so right about everything," she whispered and then lowered her eyes.

"Talk to me. Tell me about what happened. Tell me what those assholes did."

She leaned into him as he released her hand and pulled her against the dip under his arm and chest.

"They said that they didn't really love Maggie. That they used her, just like they were using me. They like sharing women."

He placed his hand against her throat and jaw, holding her firmly so she was forced to look into his eyes. She was so scared, she couldn't hold back the tears.

"You see. I told you that they were using you. They fucking killed Maggie. When Jose finds out the truth, he'll knock them off. Just like he's going to kill Luke."

"Who are Jose and Luke? Friends?"

He slowly trailed his hand down her throat and to her breast. He cupped it, and she prayed that he didn't feel the small wire and microchip thingy under the material. God, why didn't she think he would touch her intimately?

He stroked her nipple, and then cupped her harder, moving his hand along the material.

"Desi, please. We're in public."

"I don't care who sees or who's listening in. These big, plump tits are mine. No other man will ever fucking touch you again."

I don't care who sees or who is listening?
Listening? Oh shit

* * * *

"He knows. Somehow the fucker knows. We have to get her out of there," Nash stated to the agents. He looked at Riker who was straight faced with his fists by his side. They heard and they saw what he was doing to her. He was touching her, fondling her breast hard.

"We can't. We have to wait this out. They're surrounded," Commander Samone stated.

"Sir, we got the name of the one running the operation. It's Jose Ferguson. We ran a satellite image through the system to try and verify a location. We took a chance."

"And?" the commander asked the agent.

"He's in New York. He's two blocks away."

"Fucking A. We're going to get this asshole. Let's continue to monitor. Update everyone. Nash, Riker, get into position with the others."

"No, sir. We don't work for the agency anymore. We're sticking with watching over Chastity," Nash said, and Riker agreed.

"Okay. Let's do this," the commander said, and everyone moved into position.

* * * *

Chastity gripped Desi's hand as he slowly pushed his palm between her thighs. Thank God she wore jeans. If she had worn a skirt, the man's fingers would have been penetrating her by now.

"Why the jeans, Chastity? You always wear skirts and dresses." He lowered his mouth to her shoulder and neck. He must have seen the bandage there. "What's this?"

"From you, too," she whispered.

He moved his hand from between her thighs to her face, gripping her there. "Have you learned your lesson?"

"My lesson?" He squeezed harder. She gasped.

The evilness in his eyes warned her that he was out of control. Her gut instincts kicked in and she knew that she was busted. He was going to kill her. As soon as he had the chance, and as soon as he was done playing with her, he was done, and she was dead.

"I learned a lot over the last forty-eight hours," she told him.

"Like what?"

"Like men can't be trusted. Even you."

"Even me? Why wouldn't you trust me?"

"Because you lied about Maggie. You were in love with her."

Chastity was shooting from the hip right now. But last night, as she thought back about how Maggie was sent to set up Nash and Riker, and how Desi's name was on her apartment lease, she wondered if there was more to the relationship.

"I don't know what you're talking about."

"Sure you do. Nash and Riker said that she meant nothing to them. The night you beat me, and told me to leave them, you spoke about Maggie. You sounded more like a jealous lover than a friend."

He squeezed her hard, and she gasped. "You don't know what you're saying."

"Sure I do. And I'll tell you this much, Desi. I won't stay with you, give all of myself to you, unless you put her behind you, behind us. She's gone. I want, I need a man who is going to give me everything, all of him. I want to know the real you. I want to know who Jose and Luke are. I want to know who Maggie really was to you. I don't know any of these people. I don't know any of the circumstances behind your life or theirs. I only know that I'm tired of being used, of being knocked around. Can you give me that, Desi? Can you?"

He stared into her eyes, and she hoped that Nash and Riker were hearing her words. She wanted them to totally know that she had nothing to do with Desi or Maggie or the illegal activities. She was a pawn in a game. Someone caught in the middle of revenge. Nash and Riker needed to know the truth.

Desi shocked her as he pulled her closer and kissed her deeply. She could hardly breathe, never mind believe that he was making love to her mouth after her little speech. When he finally released her lips, he cupped her cheeks between his hands and held her gaze.

"You're coming with me. We're leaving the state, the country. Our life together, Chastity, begins today."

She swallowed hard as he stood up from the seat, took her hand, and escorted her out of the building. He held her hand tight as they walked down the streets. Not a soul looked their way. They moved along, and then they came to another building. Glancing around, she didn't see anyone watching, but she knew they were there. Riker and Nash promised to be there.

They got inside the dark building and approached the back area. There stood four men. There was a large amount of money on the table and their expressions were angry as he entered.

"What the fuck took you so long, and who is this?"

He shoved her into a seat. She nearly fell over.

"She's the girlfriend of the two men who killed Maggie."

"What?"

"She's mine now. They'll never see her again."

As fear and uncertainty filled her gut, Chastity heard the explosions. The room began to fill with smoke. There was yelling and chaos everywhere.

She heard the words "Freeze! FBI!" but then Desi was pulling her up from the seat and practically dragging her along with him.

"Move, Chastity."

She dug her sneakers into the flooring as they exited the building. She lost her balance, and there were men and agents everywhere. Desi shoved her to the side, between him and something hard and cold. But she stared at all the agents in shock. Her heart was pounding. She knew this was it. She could die right now. Desi held her life in his hands.

She pulled from him, and he drew a gun.

"It's over, Desi. You're done!" Nash yelled with Riker and the others pointing their guns at him.

Chastity was stuck to the side of him and a large metal pole.

Desi smiled. "She dies, just like Maggie. Live with that," Desi said then pointed his gun toward Chastity.

She didn't know what came over her, but she lunged for him, shoving him backward, giving the men the opportunity to stop him. He fired multiple times as she hit the ground. Tripping over his feet.

"Chastity!" Nash and Riker yelled.

She felt the concrete under her chest and face. Then Desi grabbed her and pulled her along the ground. One shot rang out, then a second and third. She covered her head and screamed in fear until Desi's grip loosened and then his fingers left her hair.

"Oh God, baby. What the hell were you thinking?" Nash reprimanded her.

"I love you." She crawled into his arms. He lifted her up, and she cried as Riker hugged her from behind.

"He's dead, baby. It's over," Riker whispered.

* * * *

Chastity stepped into the shower. She couldn't wait to scrub away Desi's touch. She scrubbed her teeth thoroughly, hoping to get the taste of his kiss out as well. Nash and Riker were a bit upset with her for risking her life the way she did. They told her that they needed to have a nice long discussion with her about commitment and trust. She of course told them that they should discuss it amongst one another to be sure Nash and Riker were on the same page, and then discuss it with her.

Hence, why she was now in the shower, trying to erase the day's events. She washed her hair, then rinsed it, and added conditioner. Grabbing the bodywash and loofah, Chastity began to wash away the feel of Desi's touch, the remnants of his words, his abuse, and the fact that he would never harm her again.

Nash and Riker were relieved that she was safe, and also overjoyed about finally catching the man behind the multimillion-dollar drug-smuggling operation, Jose Ferguson. Now they knew the truth about Maggie, and most importantly, that Chastity had nothing to do with any of them. It was a crazy coincidence that nearly got her killed and destroyed her almost-perfect relationship with Nash and Riker. Those two had a bit to learn about trust, themselves.

She rinsed her body clean, rinsed the conditioner from her hair, then turned off the shower, and got dried off. She was surprised that Nash and Riker hadn't joined her. Now that would be a hell of a way to celebrate. She dried her hair with the towel, her anticipation of seeing them, being with them after today, was overwhelming. It was crazy, but she missed them, and Riker and Nash somehow made her injuries less painful. She looked for her clothes to get dressed, and realized that they weren't on the counter where she left them. Someone took them.

She wrapped the towel around her body and slowly walked into the bedroom. The sight had her pausing with excitement and anticipation.

"Now what do we have here?" she asked. Riker was holding a tray of strawberries. He was completely naked. Nash sat on the side of the bed, legs wide, and tapping some kind of tube of something in his hand. The realization of what they had in mind hit her all at once.

"Take off the towel, Chastity," Nash told her.

"We're going to work on a little thing called trust," Riker added, moving toward her. He placed the tray onto the bedside table and took one ripe red strawberry off of it. He moved closer to her and traced her lips with the berry.

For such a simple move, it was erotic and sexy.

"Open up," he told her as he watched her lips. She did as she was told, enjoying this playful side of Riker. God knew, she needed for him and Nash to walk her each step of the way. She knew that they wanted to make love to her together. They spoke of very little else the entire way back to their penthouse.

But they knew that she needed the time to wash up and ease away Desi's touch. They gave her the space she needed. They placed her needs before their own, and she adored them for it.

The berry was ripe and sweet, and as the bit of juice dripped from her lips, Riker was there to lick it away and then kiss her deeply. The idea about going slow was thrown out the window. Riker lifted her up and turned her around.

As Riker stopped the kiss, she locked gazes with Nash, and he lifted her by her hips, placing her right onto his stomach. Pulling her down by her hair and neck, Nash kissed her, drawing out more of her desire with every stroke of his tongue.

She felt Riker's hands massaging her shoulders. Then they eased down over her lower back to her ass. He massaged each globe then pressed them apart and back together. The sensations stimulated her cunt, as if an imaginary line led from her ass to her pussy.

She lifted up and thrust her hips against Nash's erection. As she tried to control the kiss, Nash tugged on her hair, pulled from her mouth, and licked across her neck. He whispered into her ear, "Nice try, baby. But this is where you learn the rules." He sucked on her neck, and that sensitive little spot had a burst of cream pushing out of her pussy.

Riker stroked his finger along her pussy lips, then up over her puckered hole. He leaned down over her back and whispered into her ear as Nash pulled a nipple into his mouth.

"Oh my God!" She panted.

Riker pressed his cock over her puckered hole as he whispered into her ear.

"We're going to be one, Chastity. One unit, one team, one body and soul. We would die for you. We want you in our lives forever. You're our greatest treasure."

"Yes. Yes, I want you, too. I love you both so much."

Nash placed his hands against her cheeks. Take me inside of you. Relax this body. It's ours and we're going to take you together."

She slowly lifted up, the anticipation was incredible, yet she wasn't scared as much as she was curious. Would it hurt? Would they both fit? Would it be disappointing?

She lifted up and then lowered onto Nash's cock, taking him deeply inside of her. Tilting her head back and taking a deep breath, she held herself still a moment. The feeling of contentedness consumed her.

Riker kissed the back of her shoulder, as he reached for the tube on the bed.

"I'm going to get this sexy ass ready. I've wanted this ass since the first night I met you. The way that dress clung to your every curve. I love when you bend over. I'm planning on bending you over every goddamn piece of furniture or area I can."

"Oh." She moaned, feeling the tiny sensations erupt inside of her. Nash cupped her breasts, and as he tweaked the nipples, she felt the cool thick liquid being pressed into her anus.

"That feels weird," she said then gulped as Riker's fingers pressed into her ass next. In and out he stroked her anus with his fingers while Nash pressed slowly up and down.

"Oh yeah, oh, that feels good. I feel full, and my you-know is so sensitive," she whispered, eyes closed, as she moved atop of Nash.

"Your what feels so sensitive?" Nash asked then pulled harder on her nipples. Riker removed his fingers, and disappointment filled her. She actually moaned a complaint, and both men chuckled.

"I think she means her pussy, Nash," Riker said. She felt the top of Riker's penis at her puckered hole, then his hand on her hip.

"I have just the right thing to help you with that," Riker whispered then slowly pushed his cock into her back hole. Inch by inch, she felt the thick muscle move in deeper. Her belly tightened, her breasts tingled, her pussy gushed with cream, and then she thrust back, hard.

"Chastity!" Both men raised their voices and she lost it. She began to move back then forward then up and down. At once, both men grabbed onto her and took complete control of the lovemaking. All she could do was hold on for the ride.

They moaned, they called her name, they licked and kissed and fucked her so hard. She felt like she could lose consciousness. The sounds that filled the room aroused her entirely too much.

"Nash, harder! Riker, oh God, Riker." She didn't know whose name to call out or what she needed them to do except just not stop. *Please, God, don't let them stop.*

"Fuck, baby, you're wild." Riker growled against her ear as he gripped her hair, holding her still while he thrust one more time into her ass. He shook behind her then used his hold to turn her face slightly to the left so he could kiss her hard on the mouth.

Beneath her Nash gripped her hips and shoved up and down so fast, so deeply, she pulled from Riker's kiss to breathe. She was losing her ability to breathe. This was amazing.

Riker pulled from her ass and Nash grabbed her. Wrapping his arms around her waist, he rolled her to her back.

Her head hit the pillow, her hair scattered across the sheets, and Nash pounded into her with deep, hard strokes.

She stared up at him. He looked so intense and so wild, she clenched her teeth and admired his beauty. The thick strong muscles of his pecs shook with each thrust, and she reached up and pinched a nipple.

"Fuck. That's not fair." He yanked her hips harder against him and thrust one more time. He shook as he came and she shivered with her own release.

Then he pulled from her body, and fell flat on his stomach next to her.

"Sweet mother of God, you're a wild woman."

She felt her cheeks warm, and then Riker appeared with a washcloth and a smile.

"It appears that our Chastity truly is our very own secret treasure."

Nash ran his hands along her belly and pulled her closer to his side. He stuck his tongue out and licked her still-hard nipple.

"She sure is, and I can't wait to explore every single inch of our treasure."

She smiled then laughed as Nash began to wash her and take care of her. Like always.

Epilogue

Chastity was tired after a long night of dancing and enjoying Hidden Treasures with Nash, Riker, and their friends.

It was midnight when they left the club to head to their penthouse. She was still moving out of her apartment, but the process was slow since Nash and Riker kept her busy and with them almost all of the time. They called her their not-so-secret treasure and the key holder to their hearts.

She couldn't wait to get out of her dress and to cuddle with her men in bed. They were so caring and loving that she felt as if she had an entirely new life filled with love and pleasure.

"Chastity, we're waiting for you. We have a surprise," Nash called to her from down the hallway.

She felt all giddy inside. She loved Riker and Nash's so-called "surprises." They continuously came up with new and inventive ways to make love to her, together or separately. She especially enjoyed it when they incorporated those soft restraints. *Yowzers.*

She seductively made her way down the hallway, unzipped her dress along the way so that when she entered the room, she could make it fall softly to her feet. They would get a nice little shock when they saw the new panty and bra set she had gotten. Never mind the belly ring that was decorated with the small little dangling stars on it.

Oh yeah, tonight she would be the one to surprise them.

As Chastity entered the room, she locked gazes with Nash and Riker as her dress fell to the burgundy rug.

She placed her hands on her hips, and their eyes widened in appreciation.

"Hot damn, woman, when did you get that set?" Riker asked, swiftly approaching. He placed his hands on her hips and licked his lips. Nash came up behind her and caressed her shoulders and ass.

"When did you get the new belly ring?" Nash asked and then gently moved the thin little chains of stars back and forth across her skin.

She smiled. "I thought you two might like it."

"Oh, we like it all right, baby," Riker said then pressed his fingers under the elastic to her barely there panties and stroked her cunt.

She tilted her head back and softly moaned. She felt Nash thrust his cock against her back.

"We have a surprise for you, too," Nash whispered.

Riker pulled his fingers slowly from her pussy and then pushed her panties down her thighs. Nash held her steady as she stepped out of them.

"Come here, baby, come see the surprise," Riker said then lifted her up and against him. She straddled his waist as he walked her into the suite where candles were lit and a plush fur rug decorated the floor. She loved this room. They had spent so much time in it, to relax, to just talk, and to make love. It was just as special as the bedroom. She glanced at the fireplace, imagining what it would be like during the winter months with a large fire warming the three of them as they cuddled on the fur rug. And then she saw their surprise.

Above the fireplace was an almost identical painting of the mermaid, sitting on the boulders, slightly above the ocean, as waves crashed down over the rocks below. Her long blonde hair danced in the wind behind her. It was almost like the one they saw at the exhibit that day. The one both Nash and Riker had fallen in love with. Except in this one, there was no mistaking that the mermaid was Chastity.

Riker stared up at the painting in awe with a smile on his face, and Nash kissed her shoulder and hugged her between him and Riker.

"We fell in love with that mermaid, that painting, the day at the exhibit."

"That's when we fell in love with you, Chastity," Nash added then began to kiss her skin and caress her body.

She felt the tears reach her eyes, for she was the one who had been surprised once again, by her men, and their continued acts of love.

"I fell in love with both of you, too. It's beautiful and I love it."

"Good, because we named it after you," Riker told her.

"After me? What do you mean?"

Riker and Nash walked her closer, so she could see the artist's signature in black. It was the same painter who did the one at the exhibit. Then she saw the nameplate in gold underneath the painting.

It said, "Our Greatest Treasure, Chastity."

Chastity felt the tears roll down her cheeks. She felt the abundance of love, of belonging, and most importantly of being more than just adequate but adored. In that moment she knew and she understood what it was that was missing her entire life. True love. True love was the greatest treasure of all.

THE END

WWW.DIXIELYNNDWYER.COM

ABOUT THE AUTHOR

People seem to be more interested in my name than where I get my ideas for my stories from. So I might as well share the story behind my name with all my readers.

My momma was born and raised in New Orleans. At the age of twenty, she met and fell in love with an Irishman named Patrick Riley Dwyer. Needless to say, the family was a bit taken aback by this as they hoped she would marry a family friend. It was a modern day arranged marriage kind of thing and my momma downright refused.

Being that my momma's families were descendents of the original English speaking Southerners, they wanted the family blood line to stay pure. They were wealthy and my father's family was poor.

Despite attempts by my grandpapa to make Patrick leave and destroy the love between them, my parents married. They recently celebrated their sixtieth wedding anniversary.

I am one of six children born to Patrick and Lynn Dwyer. I am a combination of both Irish and a true Southern belle. With a name like Dixie Lynn Dwyer it's no wonder why people are curious about my name.

Just as my parents had a love story of their own, I grew up intrigued by the lifestyles of others. My imagination as well as my need to stray from the straight and narrow made me into the woman I am today.

For all titles by Dixie Lynn Dwyer, please visit
www.bookstrand.com/dixie-lynn-dwyer

Siren Publishing, Inc.
www.SirenPublishing.com

CPSIA information can be obtained
at www.ICGtesting.com
Printed in the USA
LVOW01s2247261115

464211LV00028B/1255/P